The Appointed
The Alexandra Denton Chronicles
Amanda K. Dudley-Penn

Other Books by Amanda K. Dudley-Penn

The Alexandra Denton Chronicles
The Hidden
The Appointed

The Brazil Werewolf Series
Beckoned

The Preston Vampire Series
Bound

Coming Soon

Summoned (Book 2) The Brazil Werewolf Series

I dedicate this book with so much love and affection to my youngest sister, Rosa-Ann Ruth Dudley. Thank you for your love and support.

Acknowledgments
I would like to thank my wonderful husband,
David and my children, Joshua, Isabella and Constance.
I would also like to thank my mother, Melinda "Kaye"
Hirjak and my step-father, Paul Hirjak, my step-mother,
Melinda Dudley, my grandmother, Mildred Hardy, my
father in law, Lee Penn, my mother in law, Bell Penn, my
sisters, Amber Dudley and Kara Wallace, my brothers,
Michael Dudley and James Matthews. My brother in
laws, Joe Wallace and Carl Penn. My sister in laws,
Corie Matthews, Roxanna Matthews Amanda Johnson-
Penn and Carolyne Penn, My adopted sisters, Sandra
Morris, Hopi Laliberte, Connie Sanchez and Chrystal
Ambrose, my adopted brother, Robert Sanders, my best
friend, Christina Turrentine, my aunts, Amy Russell,
Becky Dudley, Vickie Edwards, Nancy Holt, Leigh
Holland, Brenda Rollings and Connie Sekulich, my
uncles, Gary Dudley, Jason Russell, Terry Russell and
Anthony Russell, my great aunt, Peggy Russell Englant,
my cousins Catareena Taber, Lisa Anderson, Valerie
Russell, Rebecca Grieshaber, Traci Coble and
Christopher Russell and my friends, Robert Ramirez,
Jeanne Carmigle, Robert Harry, Ann Harry, Bob Rosso,
Cindy and Jason Fryman, Mandiey Hill, Brenda
Kilpatrick Paul, Andree Cornuaud, Mendy Millner,
Alexis Millner, Anna Marquez, Dominick Currie,
Trenton Carmon, Alvin Craig, Carol and Chris Foster,
Tammy Laliberte and so many more. Thank you and I
love you all.

6.

Prologue

The heat touched my skin a moment before blinking open my blue eyes.   I gasped as I took a searing breath and blinked again. The nape of my neck prickled in warning as I found myself standing on the edge of a desert cliff. A dark abyss opened below me, threatening to swallow me with one wrong move. I closed my eyes and took a deep breath once again. My head began to spin as I stood at what very well could be the gates of hell.

The one thing I didn't feel was surprise because I had expected for something to happen. It always did. When everything was going well something bad would always follow…and everything had been excellent in the five months since helping to banish my first demon back to hell with the help of my visions and a group of people like me called the Appointed.

Still, the memory of that demon was fresh in my mind, causing me to shake my head to rid myself of the fear. I couldn't think of him when every cell in my body screamed that danger surrounded me. I forced myself to focus and took another deep breath before stepping back away from the edge of the cliff. I opened my eyes again, knowing as I did I stood within a dream.

I raised my eyebrows as I took in the knowledge that I had been able to move on my own. I would not have been able to step away if I had been having a vision. I had no control of my actions when seeing the future, causing me to be a slave to my future self. I always considered that fact the most annoying part of my gift.

Still, I could not shake the sensation that I stood in no ordinary dream. I sensed it had been brought to me and not by my friend, Leighton who possessed the ability to inhabit and control other's dream worlds. Instead, I was sure someone or something dark had brought me here. The thought caused a ripple of fear to move up my spine.

"Be careful," a voice whispered to me, almost confirming my thoughts. I turned around, causing the ends of my sunshine blonde hair to whip me in the face. I frowned as I found only a barren wasteland in front of me. Only sand, tumbleweeds and the haze of heat greeted me in the distance.

My heart quickened. Something made my nerves tense, telling me this situation was not right.

I looked around again. This place was so utterly devoid of life it made me wonder when my death would come. I trembled at the thought as I squinted, trying to see into the distance as the heat stung my eyes.

"Alexandra," the voices of what seemed a thousand people whispered my name in agonized screams of torture. My mouth dried in fear as I looked around again, finally finding a hazy shadow moving closer and closer to me in the distance.

"Hello?" I called out and then, mentally kicked myself for doing so. How many times had I admonished people in horror movies for doing the same thing?

Still, the need to call out tempted me and I stifled it by pressing my lips tightly together as the shape of a person became clear. I squinted, seeing a woman within the haze walking confidently toward me. Warnings whispered through me as the prickling on the nape of my neck moved up to my scalp. My heart jumped against my chest, slamming into the ribs housing it.

I narrowed my eyes and readied myself for a fight. Although this person was a woman, I was not stupid enough to believe she couldn't be dangerous. As a matter of fact, I had learned women were usually more dangerous than men.

The woman stepped closer and closer, revealing more of herself. Her long black hair flew behind her and for a moment I wondered if this person was my best friend, Lynne but that thought faded as the woman's features became clear.

This woman's eyes were so dark they were nearly black. Her face was beautiful and exotic. Her full lips grinned with malicious intent within her tanned face. A tremor slid down my spine in warning. This woman *was* dangerous. The knowledge screamed in every cell of my body.

"Who are you?" I asked, frowning as I looked at her.

Her grin raised more but her eyes were cold as she

lifted an eyebrow at me, "You don't know?"

I shook my head, keeping my eyes firmly on her, "Why should I?"

Her eyes narrowed as she looked down her nose at me, "My name is Jezebel."

I frowned and sighed, "I don't think we've met," I said after a moment.

One side of her lips rose up again, "No, we haven't," she said as her face reddened slightly, "Though I do believe you know someone very dear to me…my lover…Asmodis. The one you killed."

Understanding hit me and I had to fight the urge to suck in a breath. She blamed me and no one else for the demise of her demon lover. I nearly laughed. I had not given him the final blow sending him back to hell. My brother, Jeremy had been the one to bring Asmodis' death. I had been dead at the time but I couldn't let her know that. I couldn't allow her to hurt him. I looked at her impassively, "So, you're a demon?"

"I am," she said, angrily.

I crossed my arms over my chest, trying to seem bored, "And you're here for revenge," I shook my head and gave a short laugh, "Well, that worked out well for Asmodis. Where is he again?" I smiled cynically as I looked straight into her eyes, "Oh yeah, he's dead."

Jezebel's face reddened further and before I had even seen her move she had pushed me and I was falling into the dark pit. I screamed in surprise and closed my eyes, willing myself to wake.

My stomach flipped as I felt my bed beneath me. I inhaled sharply and then, opened my eyes and suppressed a groan. I blinked as my room came into focus. My heart still beat hard from the fall as I wondered why I couldn't just keep my smart mouth closed. It always got me into trouble.

I sighed as my heart calmed and reached for my cell phone on the nightstand beside my bed. I dialed the number of Bastian, the protector of the Appointed. The phone rang once before Bastian answered in the broken voice of sleep.

"A demon is coming for me," I whispered into the phone, careful not to wake my sister, Kelly sleeping less than five feet from me. I realized I hadn't given him time to wake up and forced myself to stop speaking as he regained his senses.

"Alex?" He asked as sleep disappeared from his voice, "Are you sure?"

I rolled my eyes, "Of course, I'm sure," I said, exasperated, "I wouldn't call you if I wasn't. I know her name. I just don't know who she is."

Silence greeted me for a moment and I could hear the rustle of sheets as Bastian rose. A moment later, his sigh of acceptance and regret echoed over the line.

"What's her name?" He asked obviously grabbing a pen and paper on his side of the line.

"Her name is Jezebel," I said, softly.

"Jezebel?" He asked clearly confused, "I thought she was human."

"Well, apparently not," I said, frowning, "Because the woman I saw was admittedly a demon."

"Well, I suppose I won't be sleeping for the rest of the night," he said with another heavy sigh, "Do you know why she's after you?"

"Well, apparently it's because *I* killed Asmodis," I

scoffed, "She doesn't seem to know Jeremy or any of the others were involved."

"That might be a good thing," Bastian said with worry clear in his voice and then, he seemed to realize what he'd said, "I mean…we won't have to worry about anyone but you."

"I understood what you meant," I said, grinning for a moment.

"Good," he said, relieved, "I *will* find out who she is, Alex. I promise. Be careful until then."

"I will. Thanks, Bastian" I said before we said our good-byes and hung up.

Hesitantly, I laid back on my bed and stared at the ceiling. All thoughts of sleep were forgotten as the shadows stretched within the room and the first signs of daylight approached. The beginning whisper of fear worked its way into my mind as I wondered what Jezebel had planned for me. For some reason, she terrified me more than Asmodis. Maybe it was because I had been taught to fear a woman's fury more than a man's. The problem with fearing this particular woman's fury was the fact she wasn't an ordinary woman. She was a demon.

Chapter One
Plans Ruined

I paced my living room more than a little frustrated as I waited for the Appointed to arrive. My little sister, Kelly sat on the couch arm watching me with worry clearly written in her green eyes. I glanced at her as she raised her brow, knowing that she could see my frustration. Maturity older than her eleven years showed on her face. I frowned because I knew her maturity was due to the fact she had seen more than most kids her age.

After all, she was a very important member of the Appointed. She possessed the gift of healing. Unfortunately, there was a sad twist to her gift. She was not able to save everyone. Sadly, she learned that lesson when she had not been able to save our beloved protector, Reverend Boothe, who had died by Asmodis' hand.

Also, her gift caused one more problem, she was one of the favorite first targets of demons because she could cast them out of their hosts. Thankfully, no one had come for her since Asmodis and Jezebel seemed only interested in me. Still, I wondered if Jezebel would hurt Kelly or one of the others. The thought made me shiver as I thought of Reverend Boothe again. Asmodis hadn't stopped at just harming us. He had killed one of us. What made me think Jezebel wouldn't do the same?

My eyes found Kelly's again as the image of Reverend Boothe's broken body laying on the floor of his study came to me. I couldn't help but to wonder as I looked into her freckled face, if she still felt guilt over not being able to save him. Looking at her, I wouldn't be able to tell if she did. She looked well-groomed with make-up lightly covering her skin. She wore the newest clothes and her chestnut colored hair was styled in soft waves which cascaded past her shoulders. She seemed calm and collected. Still, I sensed if I looked hard enough, I would see it…I would see the guilt.

She smiled as if in encouragement when I didn't look away and I smiled back, not wanting her to worry more because of the path my thoughts had taken. I blinked and began my furious pacing once again.

"You're going to walk a hole into the floor and mom won't be happy," My seventeen year old brother, Jeremy said behind me.

I turned to find him leaning with one broad shoulder against the door frame leading from the living room to the dining room. His arms were crossed over his equally broad chest. Dark brown eyebrows were raised over eyes of the same color. One side of his full lips were lifted in a knowing crooked smile.

Out of all of the Appointed, there was something about him which proved him to be the most intelligent.

14.

The problem was he never really saw that in himself. Still, I understood why he had been given the ability to control fire. He was careful. Anyone else would have turned themselves into a blazing inferno. He had definitely been the safer choice.

"I'm worried," I said as my brows drew together. I couldn't lie to him. He would see right through it anyway.

"I know," he said, leaning up from the door frame and sitting on the couch beside Kelly. It was silent for a moment before my brother, Jonathon walked through the door.

"You shouldn't be worried," he said while towel drying his sunny blonde hair. He had recently turned fifteen years old but was already tall and lean. His green eyes sparkled as he looked at me and grinned, "We *have* kicked a demon's ass before. If she comes at you, I'll stake her with an ice sword and it will be over."

I rolled my eyes at his confidence. Jonathon controlled water. His specialty was creating ice swords and spearing demons with them. The problem was, he was nowhere near as careful as Jeremy.

"That worked out well the last time," I said, sarcastically. Jonathon made a face at me, "Besides it is really hard to defeat a demon. I died the last time we went up against one, remember?"

"That was because you went up against him by yourself," My boyfriend, Daniel said behind me. I tensed.

Daniel had the ability to transport himself from one place to the other with a thought. He had obviously done so right before my speech about defeating the demon.

I turned to him finding him standing behind me with his arms across his chest. His chocolate-brown eyes were clouded in worry. I frowned. He must have transported to my house right after waking. His wavy, dark hair wasn't even combed and his clothes were crumpled as if he had dressed in the clothes he had worn the day before.

I reached up and caressed his cheek, "I told you why I did that," I whispered, "It was the only way."

"Just don't do it again," he said, sternly as the door opened. Daniel groaned and rolled his eyes as he saw who entered.

"Did you miss me?" I heard my best friend, Lynne say as she stepped into the room, "Of course you did. You'd be crazy not to."

I shook my head and turned to see her walking in holding Bastian's hand. I grinned. They had begun to date during the summer and I believed they truly did belong together.

Lynne was gorgeous with raven black hair that shined blue in the sun and bright blue eyes. Her skin was tanned and she was built like a supermodel. Bastian was handsome with chin length blonde hair and eyes the color of the clearest, bluest ocean. He was also tall and muscular. Lynne was one of the Appointed. She had the ability to fly. Bastian was Reverend Boothe's nephew and had taken his place as our protector when Reverend Boothe had been killed. Bastian was also one of the most doting people in the world when it came to Lynne and she needed that. She deserved someone who would tell her she was as wonderful as she knew she was.

16.

"No one else is coming," Bastian said, breaking through my thoughts. I smiled softly as he yawned and continued to talk, "They either have to work or have family gatherings…well, except for Leighton. He's grounded."

"I'm glad I'm finally too old for that," Lynne said, grinning.

"Lynne, you just turned eighteen two days ago," I said, shaking my head.

Her eyes widened ignoring my comment as she looked into my face, "You look horrible," she said, frowning, "The little demon didn't let you sleep, did she?"

"Not really," I said and then, looked at Bastian, hopeful, "Did you find anything?"

He yawned again, "Yes," he said, looking very tired, "I had to get past all of the mentions of the Jezebels in the Bible but I finally found a text in Arabic."

I grinned. I still had problems imagining Bastian reading Arabic. He looked like he'd be more at home on a football field. However, he was more than adept. He was fluent in nine languages and was learning a tenth. He could also read them and he had learned every important event of just about any era in human history. Bastian was as Lynne would say super smart.

"What did you find?" Daniel asked, frowning.

"Jezebel is a lust demon," Bastian said, "And from what I understand she does her job very well."

I heard Jonathon snicker, "I'm sorry, Bastian," he said, "But I don't understand how she can cause that much trouble with lust as her power."

Bastian frowned, "Because lust isn't only sexual. You can lust after anything. You can lust for money, power or another's mate. Lust can cause people to steal, murder and it's been known to cause war."

Jonathon's eyes widened, "So, you're saying this demon *can* hurt Alex?"

"Yes," Bastian said, looking around the room, "But she hasn't found a human to possess yet and I'm sure she'll need to do that to gain any real power. So, you're safe for now."

I looked at him doubtful. Somehow, I didn't feel safe at all because to me Jezebel seemed more determined than Asmodis ever had and that made her more dangerous.

****

I was still afraid when Bastian and Lynne left. Kelly had decided to go with them so she could spend the night with Lynne. All three had assured me that I would be okay…that Jezebel wouldn't harm me but no assurances of my safety seemed to help me. Instead, they seemed to make me more frightened because they proved that no one believed I was in danger and if they didn't believe me, they wouldn't be able to protect me.

Worse, when they left I was literally alone. Though Daniel stayed, he opted to play a video game with my brothers and I never liked watching them play. Instead, I stood in the living room for a few moments trying to calm my fears as I listened to my brothers in their room arguing with Daniel over who would play first.

Honestly, my feelings were hurt. No one stayed

with me…not even Kelly who I had always counted on to be there when no one else was. My stomach clenched in fear as I realized how close I had come to begging her to stay because I could not push away the feeling that I was in terrible trouble.

I stood in the living room for a few minutes before quickly making my way to my place of peace…the deck that overlooked the large hill which made up our back lawn. Once there, I inhaled a few times, breathing deeply before releasing any of the stress from my mind.

"You're still worried," Daniel said behind me, causing me to jump. I stiffened as my heart rose into my throat and nodded my head before turning to face him.

"Yes," I whispered and took a deep, relieving breath, "I know no one believes me but I think she's going to hurt me. Somehow, she seems more dangerous than Asmodis but I don't know why I feel that way."

He walked to me and caressed my cheek, "Don't worry, Alex," he whispered, "I promise. I won't let anything happen to you."

He kissed me gently and I leaned into him, pouring everything into the kiss because fear still pounded through me and part of that fear told me I might not be with him again. Irrational or not, I trembled knowing the absolute terror of the situation would not leave my mind. Even when he left a few minutes later, there was a finality to his kiss and though I tried to tell myself that I was being ridiculous, I could not shake the feeling I was saying good-bye.

****

Even though I fought it, sleep eventually came and so did the nightmares and the visions. The worst of what reality could be, pounded through me and I awoke trembling and covered in sweat and tears.

I looked toward Kelly's bed, finding it empty. My heart jumped in my throat because for a few terrifying moments, I was unable to remember where she was. I wiped away a tear as my mind cleared and I remembered she was with Lynne.

Slowly, I took a deep breath but I could not push away the the fear and desolation. I had never been so completely alone. Worse the visions were coming back in flashing pictures which caused me to tremble. I crossed my arms over my stomach as I shook my head determined that these visions would not happen…I wouldn't let them.

I swallowed as another tear fell down my cheek. I took a deep breath and rose from my bed, needing to clear my mind of all of the horror I had seen. I walked slowly to the door and down the hall to the bathroom, as a huge lump formed in my throat. I stepped into the small room and closed the door quickly not wanting to alert my brothers or my mother.

Tears still fell down my cheeks as I looked into the mirror. My face was red and blotchy. I closed my eyes and quickly opened them because the scenes of the visions still played through my head but were jumbled and incoherent.

I remembered that Micah had been in the dream and she had been sick…very sick and there had been something about Daniel….something heartbreaking. I felt like I was going to lose him.

I shook my head again and turned on the sink, cupping my hand and allowing the cool water to fill the deep hollow to the brim before splashing it over my face. I leaned back up to brace myself on the counter, closing my eyes finding that the visions had calmed.

"Worried?" Jezebel whispered behind me, causing my eyes to open wide.

I whipped around finding her standing so close I could touch her. A wide, cocky grin stretched across her face. I opened my mouth to scream for help but saw that the action would only endanger my brothers and my mother.

"You don't want to call your family, do you?" She asked with narrowed eyes and then, she grinned, "I wonder why."

"I'll just deal with you myself," I said, straightening, "I don't need them in here for that."

Jezebel's mouth rose in a malicious smile before she whispered in my ear, "I'd rather it be just the two of us," Then, she rubbed her hands together and grinned, "This will be fun."

Before I knew what was happening, she raised her hand above her head and swiped down toward my face. I raised my arms up, trying to protect myself. A moment later, I knew I had failed as a slicing pain burned across my wrist. I lowered my arms and looked at them in shock. Four deep grooves were cut into the soft flesh. Blood poured from them.

"And it was that easy," she smiled, mocking, "I'm almost disappointed."

I took a deep breath and cried out as loud as my vocal cords would allow. Tears burned paths down my cheeks as I sank to the floor. Blood dripped down my arms and onto tile beneath my feet.

My head swam and my stomach heaved as the metallic scent of the blood reached my nostrils.   I grasped the side of the counter to hold myself steady but my knees buckled beneath me and I fell onto the hard, blood-stained tile. I moaned in pain as a knock came to the door. Jeremy's voice called to me urgently on the other side as he began to jiggle the knob. I frowned. When had I locked the door?

I opened my mouth to call out his name but only managed a whisper. Jezebel grinned above me as she dropped a knife beside me. My mind blurred and then, focused on the knife. How had it caused all of the damage with one swipe?

I watched as the blood began to surround me, spreading across the tile. It was mesmerizing to watch my life flee from me.

Jezebel stepped into my line of vision and slowly, I looked up at her, "You will understand every moment of my pain," she whispered hoarsely, "but you won't die yet, Little Alex. I'm not done with you yet."

I heard the click of the door lock and then, she was gone. Tears slid slowly down my cheeks as scenes of my visions flashed through my mind more vivid than ever. The door opened as I struggled to push them away and my brothers stood over me.

"Go get Kelly," Jeremy said, breathlessly as he stared down at me in horror.

"She's not here," Jonathon replied, pushing past Jeremy to see me. His face blanched, "She's with Lynne. We have to call the ambulance. I'll try to stop the bleeding."

An instant later, cold covered my wrists and I

knew Jonathon had frozen the wounds, "It'll stop the blood until the ambulance comes," he said before exiting the room. A few moments later I heard him screaming for my mother. Then, his voice came to me as he talked frantically to the dispatcher over the phone.

"Why did you do this, Alex?" Jeremy asked as a tear slid down his cheek.

I wanted to say I didn't but instead a vision came and I saw what would happen if I did. Instead, I began to cry and tears fell slowly down my face. My mother entered the bathroom and stifled a sob. I closed my eyes, and blocked her out by focusing on the ambulance sirens steadily growing in the distance. Jonathon came back into the room, pushing my mother back. Unbeknownst to her, he stretched forward his hand and my wrist thawed just as the medical technicians entered through the front door.

I must have passed out because it only seemed seconds later the medical technicians were leaning over me. Though they worked on me, I felt weaker and weaker. My brothers said the words attempted suicide to the man who was padding my wrists. Another tear fell. I had not tried to kill myself but it certainly looked that way. I tried to stay awake. Soon, I was lifted on a gurney.

My brother, Jeremy kissed my forehead, "Please," he whispered, "Don't do this again, Alex."

My eyelids fell closed as they lifted me into the back of the ambulance and closed the door on my life as it was…the life Jezebel had stolen from me because I couldn't think of one way that my life would go back to the way it had been.

Chapter Two
Running River

Two Months Later

I felt every moment of my stay at Running River Mental Facility. Though I was perfectly sane, the place itself nearly drove me to a level of crazy I was sure had never been introduced even within the facility's walls.

The appearance within Running River was that of a typical hospital. Everything in it was bright white. I suppose the look was meant to show how clean and sterile the place was but the odor said something else. The smell of urine and rubbing alcohol mixed causing my stomach to heave for the first few days. Though the odor faded after a while, it was still there, clinging to everything.

The inhabitants on what I'd heard the orderlies call the suicide floor was something else to be concerned with. I was sure at least half of them were there for attention. The other half were not. Oddly, I wasn't so concerned with the people who had given suicide an honest try. Instead, a deep sadness resonated in my soul for them. I wanted to help them but I had no idea how. Besides, there was always a fear I would make their depression worse and I didn't want that.

My concern rested with the ones who staged their attempted suicides because if they were willing to go to such lengths for attention, what else would they do? I shuttered at the answers my mind formulated. Those images were enough to keep me away from them, causing me to experience guilt for being grateful my roommate, Everly, had truly tried to end her life because at least I stayed safe with her.

I was also grateful that she didn't speak much. It wasn't just that I needed the quiet. More than anything it was because I was afraid of her. I'm ashamed to say that it was because of her looks I had been so timid. Everything about her seemed dark. She possessed long hair dyed the darkest black and wore black clothes. Her eyes were always surrounded in dark black eyeliner and lashes. Her skin was pale and her nails were also painted in that signature color. When I did manage to look at her, I often wondered how she had been allowed to keep her hair dyed or her make-up done. They hadn't allowed me to keep anything cosmetic besides my toothbrush and hairbrush. Still, she seemed nice enough. She often left candy on my bed and once, she told me why she had attempted to die.

It was a week after my arrival. I hadn't spoken a word to her. I think she might have been concerned for me because she asked if I was okay. Afterwards, she asked me why I had done it. Why did I try to die? When

I didn't answer, she told me her story.

She had endured what I could only call torture from her classmates. They called her names like fag, witch, freak and psycho. Her locker had been painted with these words numerous times. They also hit her or threatened her. They told her to kill herself. No teachers helped her because they thought she was a freak too. As she recounted her story, I began to see the beauty in her appearance and I felt horrible for being frightened of her. To me, she embodied strength and I wanted to be like her.

Still, we didn't talk very much after she told me her story and two months passed with the staff of the mental facility and Everly's silence my only company. No one wrote and no one visited. When the orderly came on visiting days, I always assumed he came for Everly. So, when he did call my name, I was so surprised I just stood there with my mouth hanging open.

"Alex, are you okay?" He asked, frowning in concern. I blinked, still surprised.

"Are you sure?" I asked, shifting on my feet, waiting for him to tell me that he had made a mistake but still, he didn't speak, "I mean…there's someone here to see me?"

He smiled but sympathy laced his words, "Yes, Alex," he said and I blinked again as I slowly began to believe. A slow smile stretched across my face as acceptance finally came.

"Follow me," he said, gently and I walked past Everly who smiled at me in encouragement.

The orderly didn't speak as we walked down the hallway to a small square room painted white. He motioned for me to sit at the table and exited the room. A door on the other side of the room opened only a moment later and my eyes widened as Micah and her nineteen year old son, Ky stepped in.

I winced as pain slammed through my head and I had to fight to keep from grabbing my temples. Two visions came. One had a letter that I never wished to read but would and it would break my heart. The other was of Micah laying in a hospital bed. A straight line stretched across the heart monitor. I blinked as a tremor shook me and the visions faded.

I swallowed and then, looked up meeting Micah's eyes. She was one of the Appointed, gifted with the ability to see the past by touching a person or object associated with a certain event. Still, her status as one of the Appointed did not protect her from sickness or death. Worse, I could tell she was sick. Her dark eyes had dulled and her usually beautiful black hair hung limp and lifeless. Even her usually flawless mahogany skin had paled and had darkened beneath her eyes and in her cheeks.

"Micah," I whispered as tears filled my eyes. I didn't know if I would be able to voice what I had seen. A lump had formed in my throat and refused to move.

She frowned as she sat down. Ky sat beside her and my eyes flew to him grateful for his presence. I studied him, trying to calm myself before facing Micah again. My eyes scanned over him noticing that he shared the same black hair with Micah but his eyes were beautiful and indigo in color. They were made more striking by his mahogany skin and handsome face.

He smiled sadly and then, looked into my eyes so
 intensely that for a moment, I had the uncanny thought
that he could walk through my mind and know every
secret. It was unnerving, "Hello, Alex," he said, softly.

"Hello, Ky," I said, awkwardly. I had not been
around him often but I always felt shy in his presence
though I didn't understand the reason.

"Alex you know I'm sick?" Micah asked gaining
my attention again. She frowned, studying me as my
face fell. I couldn't help but to wonder if she understood
how it would end. My heart clenched in sadness.

I nodded as a tear fell down my cheek and finally,
I was able to push the only words I could think to say
past my lips, "Micah, I'm so sorry."

She smiled and sighed, shrugging her slight
shoulders, "I've known for a little while," she said and
looked at Ky, "Though I didn't think it was so bad until
Ky began to have little flashes of my gift. Then, I knew
my fate."

"When one dies…another will take their place," I
said quoting how the gifts of the Appointed were passed
from one person to another.

"Yes," Micah whispered as tears fell from my
eyes.

"I don't see a way to fix this," I said, feeling my
heart sink in disappointment, "but there has to be."

"There's not," she said and then, sighed resigned
but when she spoke her voice was strong, "Understand
there are limits to your gift, just as there are with Kelly's
or any of the Appointed. I just wanted you to know so
you wouldn't blame yourself and do this again."

28.

My eyes widened as I realized she believed I had tried to take my life too. I almost laughed and shook my head. I couldn't let her worry about me when she was so sick. I inhaled and then, exhaled slowly before deciding what to do.

"Do you still have your gift at all?" I asked, looking into her eyes.

"I do," Micah said, frowning as she stared at me, warily, "Why?"

"Because I need for you to use it," I said, feeling my mouth go suddenly dry, "I need you to see what really happened."

"Now?" She asked obviously confused. She looked over her shoulder as if afraid someone would see.

"Yes," I said and laid my hand on the table palm up.

She inhaled and then, shook her head as she reached forward, grasping my hand. Her eyes became blank as she looked at me. Finally, her eyes opened wide as she fell further and further into my past. To anyone looking at us, they would assume she was giving comfort but I understood she was seeing exactly what had happened. Minutes passed in silence and then, a gasp escaped her and she blinked, clearing her mind.

"Oh my God," she whispered, "Alex, I'm so sorry. I can't believe that I didn't know."

Ky frowned and I looked down realizing he had been touching his mother. He had seen everything. I narrowed my eyes at him and he shrugged as if it didn't matter. The problem was that it did matter to me.

"Should I tell the others?" She asked, urgently.

"No, not yet," I whispered, "They'll find out when it's their turn."

"And you're doing this to save Daniel, even though you already know his choice?" She asked, looking heartbroken.

I nodded, "He's still one of the Appointed," I whispered, sadly, "Plus, I still...care for him."

She frowned and looked down at her hands, "Do you want the letter?" She asked in a whisper and I nodded with my heart in my throat.

She pulled it out of her jacket and handed it to me. I shook my head as I looked back at her.

"I'm sorry, Alex," she whispered, frowning over tear-filled eyes, "For everything."

"It's okay," I said and then, looked at Ky, forcing a smile, "By the way, you shouldn't have seen my past without permission. It's rude but I'll forgive you...this time."

"Sorry," he said, shifting, "I don't know all of the rules yet. We're still friends, right?"

I smiled and nodded, "Of course."

Micah watched our exchange and then, sighed relieved, "I'm glad he'll have a friend," she whispered, looking at me sadly, "He'll need one. So will his sister."

I nodded understanding that she was asking me to help them after her death. It left an odd feeling in my chest but I wouldn't deny her that comfort. I met her eyes before nodding again. She mouthed, *thank you.*

The door to the room opened and the orderly

stepped inside, "Time's up, Alex," he said almost sounding regretful.

"I'll see you when you leave in two weeks," Micah said as we stood.

I nodded my head as I stared at her for a moment, hoping she would still be alive. Tears came to my eyes but I pushed them back as I stepped forward and embraced her. I held her for a long moment as if I could hold her in life. Still, I wouldn't cry. My tears would only hurt her worse and I wouldn't do that to her.

"I love you, Micah," I said, into her shoulder.

She pulled back as she whispered hoarsely, "I love you too."

I turned and forced myself to walk through the door grasping the letter that would break my heart further. The orderly patted my shoulder.

"It's okay, Alex," he whispered, "The first visit is always hard."

I forced a smile as I looked up at him, "It can only get easier, right?"

I knew I only said it for his benefit but it seemed to work because he gave me a quick smile and nodded before leaving me at my room's door. Still, my heart was broken behind my smile. Sadly, Micah's illness wasn't the only reason. The other reason was written within the letter clutched in my hand.

****

I didn't even glance at Everly when I walked into our room but I felt her stare as I entered and I could tell she wanted to know how everything had gone. For once, she was interested in what happened to me and did not hide it. Unfortunately for her, she had chosen the wrong time to show that she cared.

I kept my head down as I shook uncontrollably. My eyes watered with tears. I went into the bathroom and closed the door without saying a word. It was rude especially since I could guess how worried she was for me. Still, I couldn't even speak of what had happened as the tears fell down my cheeks.

My eyes blurred as I looked down at the envelope, knowing what was inside. Daniel had made his decision. I wanted to scream that it wasn't the right one but I couldn't. Instead, I tried to stifle a sob. Why had I believed he would love me forever?

I closed my eyes and tore open the envelope. I took a deep, shuttering breath as I looked down and began to read.

Dear Alex,

I'm sorry. I don't know any good way to do this. I don't believe there is a good way to do this. Everyone thinks I'm being mean and reckless because of this letter. I hope you know me well enough to realize that isn't true. I also hope you understand I do love you. I always have. It's just not the same as before.

I won't lie to you and say there isn't someone else. There is. I've fallen in love with her. I tried not to but I couldn't help it. Again, I'm sorry.

I hope we can be friends. I mean, we have to work together but I hope you still care enough to be friends even though you have every right to hate me. I still care about you even though it probably doesn't seem like it.

Maybe it was just puppy love and it's run its course and now, we'll just be friends. I hope that's true. I will see you and talk to you further after you leave the hospital.

I don't know what else to say so I better go now. I am sorry.

Daniel

A tear fell down my cheek and landed on the paper, smearing the ink. Even though Daniel had confessed that he cared for me, I couldn't believe he did. He couldn't even wait to make sure I was stable before he chose to break up with me. I shook my head and then, stared at the letter as my heart shattered further. My mind ran through every moment I had spent with him only stopping when a knock sounded at the door. I blinked as I looked toward it, wondering how much time had passed.

"Alex, are you okay?" I frowned as I heard Everly's voice on the other side of the door. She really did sound worried.

I stood and cocked my head as I remembered a part of my vision, "I am now," I said, opening the door, knowing that tears still ran freely down my face.

Everly was leaning with her shoulder against the door frame and her dark grey eyes softened in sadness, "What happened?"

I shrugged, "Daniel broke up with me," I said and

her eyes narrowed as I finished the sentence, "For another girl."

"Prick!" She exclaimed, angrily.

"No, he's not," I said, still feeling the need to defend him.

She shook her head as if she didn't understand and sighed, "Can I do anything?" She asked, Sympathy coated her voice.

"As a matter of fact, you can," I said and smiled weakly.

"Okay," she said, surprised and then, threw up her hands as if helpless, "What can I do?"

"Give me a makeover," I said with raised brows.

She leaned up from the door frame and held her hands out, "Oh no," she said and scoffed, "I don't do preppy. I can't do those type of makeovers."

"I don't want a preppy makeover," I said looking into her eyes, trying to convey how serious I was, "I want to look like you."

Everly's mouth hung open in shock. She blinked twice and seemed to recover, "People will call you names," she warned me.

"I don't care," I said, raising my chin.

Everly tilted her head to the side, studying me. Finally, she nodded, "Okay," she said and then, smiled, "A me style makeover…this is something new. Usually people are asking to give *me* a makeover."

"They shouldn't. There's nothing wrong with you," I said with a smile, "Thank you for doing this."

"No need to thank me," she grinned, wickedly,

34.

"I've been wanting to bring a preppy over to the dark side for a while. This is a dream come true."

I grinned, "Well, I'm glad to oblige."

"You might want to look in the mirror and say good-bye to your old face," she said, "Because you won't be the same when I'm done with you."

My face fell in sadness as the finality of the situation hit me, "I've already said good-bye," I whispered, knowing my looks were not the only things that would change.

Chapter Three
Home

Two Weeks Later

I looked out of the one window in the room I had shared with Everly for the last two months unable to believe I was about to go home. It was strange how the last two weeks had felt like an eternity instead of just mere days. Too much had changed. I had changed.

In the two weeks that had passed, Everly had become one of my best friends, I had decided to become who I truly wanted to be and had received a makeover that had taken away any aspects of my old self. No longer did I have sunny blonde hair but black. My eyes were surrounded in ebony and my clothes and nails bore the same colors. The only thing left to me was my gift and somehow, I embraced it more than I once had.

I sighed as I glanced back at Everly who sat on the bed I was about to vacate, looking at me sadly. I smiled softly at her. In such a short time, she had become very important to me. I worried about leaving her alone.

"I wish you didn't have to go," she said poking her

bottom lip out, "You know, they're probably going to put one of the real crazies in here with me."

I blinked my now heavily lined eyelids, "I'm sorry," I said, shifting, "At this point, I wish I could stay too."

She frowned, narrowing her eyes as she studied me, "Are you nervous?"

"I am," I said and looked out of the window again before looking back at Everly.

She cocked her head to the side and smiled, "Well, you're beautiful," she grinned, "The black hair is wicked. It brings out your eyes. I love it."

"I know I'm beautiful. I look like you," I said, looking into her eyes, concerned, "Do you have my number?"

She nodded as an orderly stepped inside the room, "It's time, Alex."

I smiled at him and then, hugged Everly, "Make sure to call me as soon as you're out of here."

She gave me a lopsided grin, "Expect the call in two more weeks."

I stood and walked toward the door but turned back to her with a wide smile, "Thank you, Everly. You don't know what you've done for me."

She shrugged, "Remember," she said with a raised brow, "You fulfilled a dream of mine too. You are definitely not preppy anymore."

"No, I'm not," I laughed, "Maybe I never really was."

"Maybe not. Now go," she said wiggling her brows as she said in an ominous voice, "You're mother is waiting."

I nodded suddenly nervous again. I waved as I turned and walked out of the door away from a girl who accepted me toward people who may not be able to look past the make-up and black hair I now wore.

With every step I took down the hallway, my heart sank further and further. Tears threatened to rise in my eyes but I pushed them back down and thrust my chin out. I would not cry. I had to be strong.

"Alex, you're mother is on the other side of this door," the orderly said, softly, "Are you ready to see her?"

I took a deep breath and nodded my head, "I'm ready."

He opened the door and ushered me through the door way. My mother stood in front of me with my bags. She was the same as I remembered her. Her brown hair was perfectly combed and teased and her make-up was done precisely. Her skin was tanned and she looked thin and fit. I shifted as I realized she was going to see me for the first time with my new look and I worried about her reaction. Finally, she turned and her eyes widened as she saw me. She paled visibly.

"Alex?" She asked, stepping forward and studying my face.

"Yeah, Mom," I whispered, feeling my heart sink, "It's me."

"I didn't recognize you," she said, frowning as she reached forward and touched my hair, "What did you do to yourself?"

I knew she wasn't talking about my black hair alone. She didn't like my dark eyeliner or black lips, clothes or nails. She didn't like how I looked like a vampire and not the preppy sweet girl I had been two weeks before. Irritation flooded me.

"I changed," I said, thrusting out my chin stubbornly, "I like it."

"Oh…Okay," She stammered and looked toward the door nervously, "Maybe we should go."

"Maybe we should," I said, angry now. We walked to the door. The security guard waved, giving us a warm smile. I nodded my head once at him in acknowledgment. Then, we walked toward my mother's car.

She opened the trunk with shaking hands. I threw my bags in, feeling her gaze on me.

"Alex," she said, softly and I looked at her with a frown on my face. She took a deep breath and then, swallowed, "Are you sure you're ready to come home."

I narrowed my eyes angrily, "Yes, mom," I said, reigning in my temper, "I am."

"I'm sorry," she whispered, "I just thought I'd ask."

I nodded, "You mean because of how I look?" I asked walking to the passenger side door and waiting for her to unlock it.

She shifted as I heard the door unlock, "Yes," she whispered.

I motioned to myself with my hand, "This doesn't mean I'm suicidal."

"I just don't want to make another mistake," she said, before opening her door and getting into the car. I stood there stunned for a moment before getting in. Once I closed the door, I looked at her. Tears rested in her eyes. The anger I had been holding onto calmed and I realized that she was worried because she loved me. Everything that had happened had frightened her and she didn't want to lose me. Worse, I realized that she blamed herself.

"Mom, what happened was not your fault," I said, frowning as I felt my chest tighten, "It was mine."

Her eyes softened, "Just promise me you're okay...and I'll try to get used to your new style."

I smiled, "I'll be fine," I said and then, sighed, "And I'm sorry I hurt you."

"Don't do it again," she said, desperately and then, started the car.

"I won't," I promised playing with the bracelets that hid my scars.

She nodded, "Then, let's go home."

I took another deep breath as I prepared myself to see my siblings and the rest of the appointed. I rolled my eyes, thinking it couldn't get any worse.

****

The drive home was quiet and I often felt my mother's eyes on me as we drove through Barrington, Tennessee. I kept my face turned so I was looking out of the passenger side window. The town hadn't changed but I really hadn't expected it to because it had never changed before. Still, I pretended to be more interested than I was so I wouldn't have to look into my mother's terrified eyes and know the terror came from my appearance.

My nerves stretched as we drove through the square and down the main road before turning onto the back road that would lead us into the country. We passed a large park and two bridges before I saw my childhood home.

I studied the red brick, ranch style home as if I hadn't seen it before. It was one story with a large porch where a sizeable picture window and the front door was housed. To the left of the porch was the garage and to the right were two more windows.

There was a driveway on the far right side of the house and from that vantage point the house seemed as if it had two stories. The first story was a basement accessed by a door on the outside of the house. The second was reached by a set of stairs that led to a deck painted a rustic red. A hill full of trees and thick green foliage made up the backyard.

"Do you need help with your bags?" My mother asked, interrupting my study of the house I would always call my home.

I looked at her, tilting my head to the side before answering, "No, I think I can manage."

She nodded and whispered, "Okay."

I forced a smile and got out of the car. My mother opened the trunk and I grabbed my bags before walking to the front of the house. I opened the door and shook my head. No one locked their doors in Barrington which I had always thought was crazy. I stepped inside and looked up.

Every single one of the Appointed stood within the room gaping at me. I didn't smile nor did I move. Their eyes drifted over me as I flushed and shifted uncomfortably.

"Hi," I said after a few moments and then, threw my hands up in frustration, "I'm home."

Finally, Micah stepped forward and hugged me

before whispering, "Welcome back, Alex."

"Thank you," I said, smiling sadly at her. She patted my cheek before she moved away.

Ky came up to me next and hugged me gently, "Don't take offense to this, Alex but you're hot," he whispered in my ear.

I blushed, "Thanks."

The others still stood with their mouths hanging opened, "It's still me," I said, frowning at their reaction, "I'm not going to kill you or anything like that."

Finally, Lynne blinked and then, looked around, "Of course it's still you," she said in her usual bossy tone, "Do you need help with your bags?"

I shook my head but still, I was grateful when everyone moved and I walked past them to my room. I could be alone for a few seconds even if it was only to set my bags down. I took a few deep breaths and returned to the living room.

I watched quietly as everyone talked. None of them had noticed my return. I took a deep breath realizing they wouldn't miss me for a few moments.

I walked back through the door leading to the dining room as quietly as I could and walked across the room to the sliding glass door. I pulled it open and stepped outside onto the deck.

I inhaled deeply. I hadn't been home five minutes and already I felt claustrophobic. I inhaled again taking in the air and feeling at peace. Unfortuanately, the peace ended when I turned to find Daniel standing outside the door. In an instant pain slammed into my chest and grabbed my heart in a death grip. A lump formed in my throat and I sensed the tears beginning to burn my eyes. It took a great effort but I raised my chin and narrowed my eyes to cover the hurt.

"Alex," he said, gazing at me from head to toe, "Did you do this because of me?"

I narrowed my eyes further, "Don't be conceited," I said, raising my chin, "I did this because I like it."

He shifted nervously and my heart clenched again, "I didn't mean for it to sound that way. I just feel-"

"Guilty?" I asked and then rolled my eyes, "You should."

"I still care about you," he whispered and I laughed.

"Whatever," I said, tilting my head as I studied him, "If you cared you would have stood by me. You didn't."

He blanched, "If you cared about me or anyone else, you wouldn't have tried to die," I raised an eyebrow when he flinched at his own words. His voice was softer when he spoke again, "Why did you do it, Alex?"

"It's not your concern," I said and then, shrugged as if I didn't care about him or what he thought, "*I'm* not your concern...not anymore."

"I thought we would be friends," He whispered, shifting again.

I shook my head, trying to fight tears, "No thanks."

Hurt slammed into his eyes and I had to fight to continue to look at him, "We're still members of the Appointed."

I scoffed, "Since that seems to be what is really worrying you, I'll promise you this...I will still protect you from the demons but I do not need to be your friend to do that. Now, will you please leave me alone."

He shifted again on his feet and turned. Just before entering, he stopped, "I'm sorry, Alex. I really am."

Then, he was gone. Tears filled my, eyes threatening to spill over as Ky stepped onto the deck. He frowned as he looked into my eyes.

"Are you okay?" He asked, concerned.

"I was taking care of an ex," I whispered as I looked up at him, "He seems to think I should still be his friend. We have differing opinions."

"Well, that sucks," he said and then, smiled softly, "I just came out here to compliment your t-shirt."

I frowned and looked down to see that the same cross and pistols on my shirt decorated his. I looked up at him and grinned, "Thanks. It seems you have the same bad taste as me."

He frowned and then, understanding dawned in his eyes, "I wouldn't call it bad taste," He said, leaning back against the railing, "I guess everyone has been giving you a hard time about how you look."

I nodded, "My mom so far and Daniel seems to think I did this because of him. Sadly, I know the others will follow," I said, shrugging.

"Well, before you face them," He said leaning up and walking to the door, "I meant it when I said I think you look hot."

He looked back at me and wiggled his brows before stepping inside. I laughed as the anger and hurt I had felt at seeing Daniel faded. I was only left with warmth. I watched Ky feeling as if I might have a friend after all.

Chapter Four
Facing the Truth

My welcome home party died down soon after it began. Honestly, I didn't understand how it was my party when no one spoke to me. As a matter of fact, many of the Appointed made a hasty retreat just a few minutes after I had returned to the living room.

Instead of brooding on that fact, I sat on the couch while everyone else talked. The only attention I received was when they would look in my direction for brief moments before turning back to their own conversations. I knew that part of their avoidance was because of what had happened. They believed that I was the crazy girl who had tried to commit suicide. To them, I was fragile.

Still, the isolation left me feeling strangely hollow. I couldn't help but to think that if I had disappeared, no one would have known.

After an hour of no one speaking to me, I stood and walked to the deck. I couldn't sit there anymore because all it did was cause me to feel more miserable. However, I soon found I was wrong in my assumption that no one would notice my absence.

"Are you hiding?" Ky asked, causing me to turn. He stood just outside the sliding glass door with his grin widening on his face.

I shifted as if I had just been busted doing something wrong but when I looked into his eyes, I saw the mischievous glint there. I sighed, relaxing.

"Well…yes," I said, laughing as I motioned toward the door, "Obviously, no one else is going to realize I'm gone."

He looked over his shoulder and frowned before shaking his head. He looked back at me with sympathy clear on his face.

"Yeah, I don't understand that," he said, frowning.

I shrugged and then, bit my lip, unsure what to say. Only noises coming from the side of the house broke the uncomfortable silence. Ky and I turned in time to see Catherine walking with Jace to his car. They hadn't even searched me out to say good-bye. A sliver of hurt pierced my heart.

Ky nudged me with an elbow, obviously trying to take my attention off of them, "Hey," he said, grinning down at me, "Don't worry about them. They'll remember how important you are."

I pursed my lips, "I doubt it."

He frowned and tilted his head, "Why do you say that?"

"Because I'm not that important," I whispered as I watched Leighton, Sarah and Jenna walk to Leighton's car. Jenna stopped and looked up at me with a confused frown on her face and waved just before she got in.

"No one understands their importance," Ky said and I turned back to him with a frown still marking my face as he continued, "But I do understand yours."

"You do, do you?" I asked raising my eyebrow.

He nodded, "You are important to this group though they're being too shallow now to realize it. You're important to your family and you're important to me."

I shifted feeling as if he was wrong but I couldn't voice it, "Thanks."

"No problem," He said, standing beside me as I looked out over the back yard. The shadows were shifting and it was quickly becoming night. Ky stood quietly beside me allowing me to think in silence.

The silence was only broken when I heard my brother Jonathon's voice sound behind me, "There you are," he said, exasperated, "Everyone has left except for Micah and Ky."

I turned to him and saw his face redden in anger, "I know," I said, frowning, "I saw a few of them leave."

"And you didn't come out to say good-bye. You don't leave your own party, Alex," Jonathon said, thrusting out his chin. I saw Micah, Kelly and Jeremy step out on the porch behind him.

"Jonathon, don't," Kelly said, frightened. Her eyes widened as she looked at me and I knew she was afraid of what I would do to myself if pushed.

"Well, she doesn't care about anyone but herself," he said, looking into my eyes, "She'd rather spend time with someone she barely knows than us."

I winced and raised my chin, "Ky is one of the Appointed now."

"Only because someone is dying," he said, narrowing his eyes at Ky as if Micah's impending death was his fault.

I watched Micah blanch, "All of us are Appointed because someone died," I pointed out quickly.

Jeremy stepped forward, "Jonathon, don't do this," he whispered before turning to me with pleading eyes, "I guess we're all upset. I mean…I don't understand the way you look and I don't understand why…you did what you did."

I laughed but it was hard and bitter, "You don't know anything."

"Then, tell me what happened," he pleaded. I looked at him more than a little hurt.

"How about I show you?" I asked. I lifted my hand ready to use one of my gifts. I had found a way to show the others what my visions were without even speaking . Thankfully, the gift also showed my memories.

I closed my eyes putting that part of my past firmly in my mind. Slowly, I put my hand to my lips and blew out like I was blowing a kiss. Light poured from my lips, flying through the air past Ky and Micah until it reached my siblings. I heard Ky gasp as the light was breathed into my brothers' and sister's nostrils. Their eyes closed for a few moments and when they opened their eyelids, light poured from their eyes.

I waited as the light dimmed and they stared at me in shock. Jonathon stood still for a moment before he walked to me and hugged me hard.

"I'm sorry, Alex," he whispered as I felt his hot tears on my shoulder, "I should have known that you wouldn't try to leave us."

"We all should have known that Alex wouldn't do that," Jeremy said and then, looked from Ky to Micah, "You both knew?"

"She told us not to tell you," Ky said with his hands out as if defending himself.

"You had to find out now," I said, frowning, "*I* had to tell you."

Jonathon nodded his head, "So what do we do?"

"That's where it gets complicated," I said, looking worried, "Do you trust me?"

Jonathon as well as Kelly and Jeremy nodded their heads, "Of course, we do."

I smiled relieved because for the first time in two and a half months, I didn't feel alone.

****

I laid in bed feeling better. Not everyone knew I hadn't tried to take my life but at least my siblings, Micah and Ky knew. I wasn't alone anymore. Still, there were the worries of Jezebel and Daniel. Daniel stood to lose not only his life but his soul and I couldn't let that happen…no matter what he had done to me. Still, I couldn't deny that relief flooded me at the thought that there would a better chance he would be saved and that made me relax. Sadly, I understood the reason why. I still loved him.

I sighed, closing my eyes, finally at ease.
Everything was coming together and I could rest without
worry.

I don't know how much time passed when the door
to my room opened. I frowned as I opened my eyes and
looked at the bed beside mine thinking Kelly had gotten
up but I found she still slept peacefully. I glanced back,
finding no one. Slowly, I rose, walking half-way across
the room and stood at the foot of Kelly's bed. My hand
rose and I knocked twice on the wall, trying to get my
brother's attention on the other side. On the third knock
the wall cracked down the middle, My eyes widened in
fear. It took a moment to realize that I was in a dream. I
tensed waiting for Jezebel. I was sure she would arrive
any moment to taunt me or to hurt me again.

I took a deep breath and reminded myself that she
couldn't hurt me in a dream but we hadn't thought she
could hurt me without a host either. I swallowed as I
wondered if I would die on my first night back. Fear
tried to engulf me but I knew that I couldn't let it.
Slowly, I lifted my chin ready for the battle of wits I was
sure to face.

"Where are you?" I asked, looking around. I
narrowed my eyes as a wind of pure heat swept past me.

A tremble shook me, betraying me and showing
my fear as I looked around the room. I tensed as the
walls began to crumble and fall around me. I blinked and
when I opened my eyes the room was gone. Everything
was gone.

The earth quaked beneath me and I jumped back as
a large pit opened before me. My eyes widened as I seen
a lake of fire screaming with the souls of millions. I

winced when I realized they called my name. I
scrambled further back.

"You need to step away from the pit," A man's
voice said, behind me and I turned quickly realizing I
was once again in the barren wasteland where I had first
met Jezebel. My eyes widened as I stared into the
handsome face of an angel. I blinked thinking I was
mistaken but still his snow white wings stretched behind
him. His silky black hair blew around his face, whipping
against the feathers. His eyes were a bright, vivid green.
He had the body of a warrior and he held a sword which
seemed made of crystal but white flames shot from it
along the edges.

"Who are you?" I asked frowning.

"My name is Semarias," he said, pursing his lips
for a moment as he looked past me at the pit.

"You aren't a demon?" I asked, still unsure.

"No," He said with disgust clearly written on his
face and then, looked back at me, "I'm an angel sent to
help you."

"Help me do what?" I asked with wide eyes, "Die?
You nearly gave me a heart attack."

He frowned as if confused and then, smiled. I
blinked, dazzled as he spoke, "I didn't mean to frighten
you."

I shook my head, "You didn't think that the earth
falling away under my feet and causing a big pit into hell
wouldn't frighten me?"

"I didn't choose the place," he said, defensively as
he lost his smile, "I only showed up."

I shook my head again, realizing we were getting
nowhere, "Why are you here, Semarias?"

"I am supposed to close Jezebel's portal when she is sent back to hell," he said, motioning to the pit as if I should have already known. I narrowed my eyes at him.

"Why can't *you* send her back to hell?" I asked, confused, "I mean…you are an angel. Surely, you can fight her better than a mere mortal."

Semerias laughed at me like I being was ridiculous, "Because she is meant to be defeated by one of the Appointed," he said with a smirk, "And you are meant to figure out who that is."

I pressed my lips tightly together feeling more than a little annoyed, "Can't you tell me?" I asked, angrily.

"No. I don't know who it is but *you* do," he said, raising his thick, dark brows, "Use your gift. The answer is there and when you find that answer, Jezebel will be defeated and I will be here to seal her fate."

I nodded and he was gone as quickly as he'd come. In an instant, I was no longer in the desert wasteland. Instead, I lay in my bed in my room with my eyes opened. I frowned unable to remember waking up. Yet, I had. Worse, I was positive I had been visited by an angel and it had not been just a dream. I sighed and shook my head as I looked up at the ceiling and silently asked the same question I had always asked. Why me?

When no answer came I pursed my lips and closed my eyes forcing visions to come to me as I searched for the one who was meant to defeat Jezebel.

Chapter Five
Confrontation

The insistent ringing of my phone woke me at eight O' clock the next morning. I glared at it before picking it up and saying a very groggy hello.

"Wow, glad you're such a morning person," I heard Ky say on the other end of the line.

"Yes, I love mornings so much that I'm plotting your murder," I said with my eyes still closed. For a moment, I wondered why I had given him my number, "What do you want?"

"I want you to get up!" He said brightly. I threw my free arm over my eyes.

"What for?" I whined and I heard him chuckle. I groaned angrily.

"Because you need to get out of those four walls especially since you just got out of the hospital," he said and then, paused, "Besides, I need someone to help me find some books for mom since I don't read if I can help it."

I smiled, "So, you need a bookworm."

He laughed, "Yes," he said, "So, will you go with me."

I groaned again and sat up, "Yes, I'll go. Just give me ten minutes."

"Okay," he said, "I'll be there in five."

"You suck," I said as he hung up.

Kelly opened her eyes to look at me with confusion written clearly on her face, "What's wrong?"

"Nothing," I said and then, sighed, "But I will be gone for a while today."

Her frown deepened, "With whom?"

I shrugged as if it didn't matter, "Ky."

She grinned as she sat up, "You're hanging out with him alone?," she asked, raising her brow, "Do you like him?"

"Not the way you're implying," I said, squirming. For some reason, the question made me uncomfortable, "He's my friend."

"Your friend," she said as if she didn't believe me, "He's an awfully cute *friend*."

I shook my head, refusing to look back at her as I headed to the bathroom. I brushed my teeth and put on my make-up before going back to my room to dress. Kelly looked at me with raised brows as I put on pair of black jeans with silver zippers placed in multiple places along the sides and the legs. I picked a black band t-shirt. Finally, I grabbed some socks and my military style boots and began to pull them on my feet.

"You do know he's already here," Kelly said,

watching me.

I looked up at her and frowned, "No, I didn't know," I said and then, smiled widely, "How long has he been here?"

"About ten minutes," she said and then, shrugged as she watched me put on my boots, "I figured he could wait."

I grinned as I rose and ruffled her hair, "Yes, he can," I said and kissed her on top of her head, "I'll be back in a little while."

"Be careful," she said. I could see the worry clear on her face.

"I will," I said, smiling sadly, "I promise."

She nodded as I exited our room and walked down the hallway into the living room. Ky stood there as handsome as ever and staring out of the picture window. The sun rise was beautiful beyond the mountains and I stopped for a moment to study it before turning to him.

"Are you ready to go?" I asked and he looked down at me and grinned.

"Not really," he said and shrugged, "Looking for books is just not my idea of a way to spend a Saturday."

"It's for your mom," I said and his eyes darkened.

"I know," he replied and shrugged uncomfortable, "That's why I'm doing it."

I grinned, "Then, let's go."

He led me to a black muscle car probably made in the sixties. It looked large and mean. I pursed my lips. This was exactly the type of car I had expected for Ky to drive.

"Do you like it?" He asked, proudly.

"Yes," I said, sliding my hand over the black hood,

"It's beautiful."

"She's my baby," he said, raising his brows as I got in.

"I can understand why," I said with a small smile.

I reached the passenger side door and opened it, getting in. The interior smelled of gasoline and motor oil. It was obvious Ky spent a lot of time fixing the car. I fastened my seatbelt as I watched him get in and start the car with a flourish. He looked at me and grinned.

"Hang on," he said, putting the car into reverse and backed out of the driveway.

I was about to ask him why I should hold on when he put the car into drive. A second later, my head was thrown back into the head rest. My eyes widened in fear.

"Slow down! Slow down! Slow down!" I screamed in terror. Ky laughed as we sped down the nearly deserted highway. My heart leapt into my throat as we passed the park and the bridge. Two minutes later we pulled onto the main road. Only then did he slow.

I hit him across the shoulder three times. Still, he laughed, "What are you…a psycho?" I asked angrily, "Were you trying to kill us?"

He laughed, "No," he said breathlessly, "I was having fun. You do remember how to have fun, don't you?"

I pursed my lips, "Yes."

"Good," he said, pulling into the book store parking lot. I stared out of the window and smiled. The bookstore in Barrington was surprisingly large. It was located on the main road and was as big as two large grocery stores. It was also one of my favorite places.

We walked in looking toward the cashier as we

walked past her. She looked at us nervously before returning her gaze to her book. I narrowed my eyes at her before walking down the aisle directly in front of us knowing that she was afraid of how I looked.

I pushed the anger away and then, looked around before my eyes landed back on Ky, "What kind of books does she like?" I asked, frowning.

He made a face, "Romance," he said, "Honestly, I don't know why women read that stuff."

"Because men fail to give us the things we need," I said, with raised brows.

He stepped close to me, grinning when I backed away. His face was an inch from mine, "And what is it that you need, Alex?"

I pushed his chest, "Right now, I need some space," I said, giving him a small smile and hoping that my remark didn't hurt him too bad.

He backed away with his hands in the air, "Whatever you need, Alex," he grinned, "But damn my bad luck with women."

"Maybe you should read a romance," I grinned at his look of disgust.

"No, thank you," he said, rolling his eyes.

"Or you could let a girl sleep in on the weekend before her first day back at school after a supposed attempted suicide," I said narrowing my eyes in mock anger.

"I don't think that will help either," he said as the bell above the shop door rang.

"I do," I said, pouting.

I turned and walked toward the romance section and picked up two books. I handed them to Ky, "These should do," I said, grinning.

He rolled his eyes again as he looked down at the covers of the heroes holding their heroines in exaggerated romantic scenes. I walked past him as he stared down at the covers to walk to the next aisle. I turned the corner, still looking at Ky and ran right into a girl of about my age, knocking her to the ground.

I blinked in surprise as the girl looked up at me with beautiful brown eyes. She nervously swept her caramel colored hair behind her ears before she began to stand. I stretched out my hand and she took it, grateful and got to her feet.

"I'm so sorry," I said, softly as the girl smiled, "Are you okay?"

"Alex!" I heard Daniel's familiar voice. There was a note of panic. I turned to him, frowning, "What do you think you're doing?"

I stared at him confused, "I was just walking," I said, frowning, "I bumped into her. So, I was apologizing."

I blinked trying to understand his anger. He grabbed the girl's hand and she cuddled close to him. Understanding entered my mind. She was the girl he had left me for.

"So, this is your friend Alex?" The girl asked with wide innocent eyes, "I'm Renee Fairwell."

I looked at Daniel as my face reddened in anger. He hadn't told her about our relationship.

"My name is Alex but I'm not Daniel's friend," I said, shaking my head at him, "I've found he's less than honest in some situations."

I felt Ky step behind me and stop. Daniel's eyes

narrowed as he looked at him. Tension crackled through the air.

"Ky," he said, tightly, "You've been keeping Alex company a lot lately."

Ky frowned, "We're friends," he said, stepping closer to me as if trying to reassure me that he was there if I needed him.

"Yes, and now I would like to leave with my friend," I said, glancing toward the door. I looked at Renee, "It was nice to meet you."

She nodded her head still confused and blinked, "It was nice to meet you too," she said, furrowing her brow.

I turned and walked out of the door. Ky stopped at the counter to pay for the books and joined me. I looked down at my combat boots studying them for a moment.

"Was that the girl he cheated on you with?" He asked, quietly.

"Yes," I said and looked back toward the book store as we walked toward the car, "I don't think she knew."

"Daniel's such a prick for this," he said, frowning.

I shrugged, "She was pretty."

Ky stepped in front of me and tilted my chin up by touching it with his fingertips. He looked into my eyes and then, shook his head.

"She doesn't compare," He said before he turned and continued to walk toward the car.

I smiled, feeling a dangerous tightening around my heart.

****

Ky had received a call from Micah right after we left the bookstore asking him to come home. He looked at me apologetic and I smiled, hoping to make him feel better about leaving.

"I would ask if you would like to come with me but she doesn't sound as if she feels well," he said, sadly. I frowned as I experienced the need to reach forward and caress his cheek. Instead, I curled my hand up in my lap, wondering how he was having such a strong affect on me.

"It's okay," I said as worry entered my heart for Micah but also for him, "You need to be with your mother."

He glanced at me with tears resting in his eyes, "Yes, I do," he whispered in a husky voice ripe with tears, "Thank you for understanding."

I nodded. He drove in silence until we reached my house. I looked at him, feeling his sadness resonate through me, "If you need me, call me."

He smiled but a tear fell down his cheek, "Of course."

I got out of the car, closing the door behind me. I didn't look back because I was afraid if I did, I would run back to him. That thought frightened me. I was beginning to care too much about him.

Instead, I forced myself to walk toward the front of my house, glancing back only when he was driving away. I stared after him sensing my heart in my throat.

A few moments passed before I couldn't see him anymore. I was alone…or so I thought.

"Alex," I frowned as I focused on the voice that had spoken my name. Immediately, my mind was no longer on Ky. Slowly, I closed my eyes. The voice itself brought images of my mother's bruised face. Instantly, love and hate swamped me.

I turned to see my mother's ex-husband, my step-father standing on my porch. His dark hair shined in the sun. His green eyes sparked with an emotion I assumed he had lost for me...love. My heart squeezed as I looked at the man who I had once thought was my father.

"Bradley?" I asked frowning as I stepped closer to him. For a moment, I wondered if my mother knew he was standing on her porch.

"I remember a time when you called me daddy," he whispered, looking hurt.

"I haven't seen you in seven years," I said, raising my chin, "Things tend to change in that period of time."

He smiled sadly, "I want you to remember that," he said with a sigh.

I glanced at the driveway, noticing the absence of my mother's car, "Does mom know you're here?"

He smiled but the sadness remained in his eyes, "Yes," he said and then stepped off the porch so that he wasn't towering over me, "I talked to her this morning."

"You've talked to mom?" I asked with wide eyes, "You and her aren't-"

"No," he laughed nervously, "I don't think that will ever be an option after how I treated her."

I nodded, relieved, "It's really not," I said. My mother had a new life with her boyfriend, Andrew. She really didn't need to go back to her old one.

I glanced at him and winced. It was hard to look at this man who I loved so much but who reminded me of a fear so great it still shook me. I still remembered fearing for my mother's life.

"Alex, I've asked for her forgiveness," he said,

softly, "I hope you will forgive me too."

I bit my bottom lip. The truth was that I wanted to forgive him but my memories wouldn't let me. I still remembered every punch he had bestowed on my mother. I pushed those images away as quickly as I could and looked at Bradley again.

"What about my brothers and sister?" I asked, narrowing my eyes, "Have you asked for their forgiveness?"

"Yes," he said and my mouth dropped open in shock. No one had told me.

"What have they decided to do?" I asked, hurt that I was once again left in the dark. Bradley shifted suddenly uncomfortable.

"Kelly is more accepting but Jeremy and Jonathon are going to try," he said, tilting his head to the side, "I know it will be more difficult for you because you remember."

More images assaulted my mind, "Yes, I do," I whispered, trying to replace those images with the images of Bradley teaching me to ride my bike or taking me fishing, "But I remember the other things too."

He closed his eyes and breathed out slowly, "I'm glad," he said and opened his eyes.

I stepped closer to him, tilting my head as I studied him, "Why are you asking for my forgiveness now?"

A frown crossed his brow and tears welled up in his green eyes, "I heard what you did," he said, choking over a sob, "And I wondered if you did it because of what…I did."

I shook my head and then, stared at him trying to construct an answer. Finally, I sighed, "I don't know why I did it," I whispered and looked into his eyes, "but I can promise that it had nothing to do with you."

He nodded but I could tell that he didn't quite believe me, "I am sorry for what I have done in the past," He said, sniffling, "If there is anything I can do to make this easier or to gain your forgiveness then let me know."

I stepped forward and hugged him as my soul released a part of my past I had never hoped to let go of.

"I forgive you," I whispered and Bradley cried even harder as he hugged me back.

"Thank you," he cried into my shoulder.

I nodded unable to say anything else. Instead, I took a deep breath as the darkness in my soul began to fade.

****

After Bradley left, I couldn't bring myself to enter my house. No one was home and I didn't want to be there alone. I turned and began a walk I had not taken since just before Jezebel's attack.

The gravel road to the dock where I had sat so many times with my brothers or Lynne and even Daniel still seemed the same. It was relieving to know that it hadn't changed. I took a deep breath and for once I believed everything would be okay.

That was until I saw Jezebel standing in the middle of the dock smiling at me. I narrowed my eyes at her and continued to walk toward where she stood. I could not remember when I had learned to push fear away but I had. Still, I was cautious and stopped well away from her at the top of the dock's bridge.

"Are you here to give me more scars?" I asked standing on the edge of the entrance of the dock. I placed my hands on the ropes on either side of the wooden entrance posts looking down the dock bridge at Jezebel with my face reddening in anger.

She shrugged as she stepped to stand at the other side of the dock bridge. Ten feet separated us. Still, I didn't move.

She smiled, "Now, why would I scar you when my host can do so much more damage to you than I?" She asked and laughed.

I narrowed my eyes. So, she had found someone to possess while I was away. I wondered briefly who it was.

"If you have possessed someone, why are you here alone?" I asked, frowning.

"Well, she's asleep right now," she said, with a half grin, "And I was concerned and wanted to see how you were doing since you are the town crazy that tried to commit suicide and then, went all emo or goth."

"I'm doing wonderful," I said, sarcastically, "So, since you know, why don't you go back to hell where you belong."

"I think I'll stay because I am positive I can do worse than those scars on your wrist," she said, laughing. Then, she raised her brows, "Do they remind you of me every time you see them?"

I raised my chin as my face burning with anger, "They remind me that I want to kill you," I said with narrowed eyes, "And I will…just like I killed Asmodis."

Jezebel stepped forward threatening me with every move she made. A moment before reaching me, Catherine's sweet voice sounded behind me.

"You feel the flames of hell burning your skin,"

she whispered and Jezebel's eyes widened as pain slammed into their dark depths, "You see the flames. You smell and taste the sulfur."

Jezebel screamed out as I turned to face my friend. Her strawberry blonde hair blew behind her and her blue-green eyes narrowed in anger.

"Stop," Catherine said and Jezebel sank to her knees panting. Catherine raised one eyebrow as she stared at the demon. Jezebel pulled herself to stand and a moment later disappeared.

I blinked as Catherine looked at me. No one would suspect the dark gift she had. She controlled other people's senses. If Catherine wanted to, she could make you believe you were on fire. You would see the fire as if it was right in front of you. The heat would sear your skin and the pain it caused would be real. The stench of sulfur would enter your nose as would the smell of your burning flesh. You would hear the crackling of the flames. You would truly believe you were on fire. Thankfully, Catherine was too sweet to use her gift in such a way on humans. Obviously, she didn't have the same restraint for demons.

"How did you know?" I asked, wondering how she knew where I was.

She shrugged and pointed at her boyfriend, Jace running toward us. He was tanned and blonde with blue eyes. I had always thought he looked more like a surfer than someone born and raised in Tennessee. He was also one of the Appointed. He could read minds. Obviously, he had used his gift.

"You scared me half to death, Catherine," he said, panting. He looked at me with narrowed eyes, "And you've been hiding things from me. Remind me to thank Gloria for showing you how to hide your thoughts."

I shrugged, "Sorry," I said when he continued to stare at me.

"Would you please explain to us what is going on?" He asked, putting his hands on his knees and panting some more.

I closed my eyes and took a deep breath, "It will be easier to show you."

He winced, "No offense, Alex but that extra little gift of yours always freaks me out."

"Well, it's the only way to tell you," I said, angrily.

"I could read your mind," he said with raised brows.

I shook my head, "That freaks *me* out."

He nodded with narrowed eyes, "Okay," he sighed resigned, "Do it."

I looked at Catherine and she nodded her head. I closed my eyes and put the dream before Jezebel's attack and everything after that into my mind. Slowly, I rose my hand and blew out. The light blew out brighter and brighter from between my lips. Finally, the stream of light reached them…twisting and twirling before entering their nostrils. Catherine gasped after a few moments and then, opened her eyes. Jace soon followed. The light poured from their eyes and dimmed. Finally, they blinked and everything was normal again.

"Are you sure this is how it needs to happen?" Jace asked, looking at Catherine worried.

"I'm positive," I said, smiling.

66.

"I'll do anything you need," Catherine said with a shrug, "Just don't hide anything from us anymore."

"I won't," I whispered, shifting uncomfortably.

"Alex, I'm sorry for treating you so badly," she said and then, looked back at Jace.

He nodded, "I am too."

"Don't worry about it," I said, and then, shrugged, "We have other things to worry about.

Jace nodded his head, "And other people."

He looked from Catherine to me with fear written clearly in his eyes. Sadly, I couldn't promise that everything would be okay.

Chapter Six
Historic

Catherine paced in front of me with her hands clasped in a firm grip behind her back. She stopped after a few minutes and turned to look at me with wide eyes. I shifted uncomfortable in her steady gaze. She frowned and walked to the picture window and looked out at the mountains in the distance as if in deep thought. Slowly, she turned to me again with an expression so sad my heart ached.

"Are you sure you can't just tell Daniel?" Catherine asked after a few moments of silence, "I mean...he may believe you."

I frowned and shook my head, "You saw what

would happen if I do that," I said with a shrug, "He will die and he will lose his soul."

She sighed deeply and pinched the bridge of her nose between her thumb and forefinger.

"Honestly, I don't know why you're even bothering," Catherine said, tilting her head, "He didn't exactly treat you right."

"No, he didn't," I said, closing my eyes as the pain in my heart spread. I took a deep breath and bowed my head. Perhaps, I had mistaken the sadness for sympathy. Slowly, I let the air release from my lungs as I opened my eyes and turned to her again. I shrugged and continued, "But it's different. We've known each other our whole lives. I can't ignore that."

"He shouldn't have treated you that way," she said, as her face paled in grief, "None of us should have, but what he did was worse."

My eyes widened and I suddenly realized her grief was for what she had done. The sympathy was for how I felt. I reached forward and touched her arm in comfort.

"What if Jace did the same thing?" I asked after a few moments.

Her eyes softened and she nodded her head slightly, "I would be willing to do everything to keep him safe."

"Then, you know how I feel," I said with a small, sad smile.

"Yes, I do," she whispered. A frown creased her brow and more sympathy flooded her face, "So, what about Ky?"

"What about Ky?" I asked with narrowed eyes even though I knew what she would say before she said it. Still, I hoped she wouldn't voice what was on her mind.

Catherine pressed her lips together and shook her head. Then, her eyes met mine, "Alex, anyone can see that you are starting to feel something for him," she said and threw her hands up, "You are around him all of the time."

I shifted uncomfortably, "He's my friend," I said even though it was a lie. He was beginning to be more than that and it scared me more than anything...even Jezebel, "He's the only friend I've had."

She covered her eyes quickly trying to hide the hurt but I had already seen her flinch as the words left my mouth. When she looked at me again, she raised her brows.

"You're afraid," Catherine said but smiled softly as she patted my shoulder, "That's alright. I understand why."

I stared at her in silence. She turned and once again looked out of the window as if the conversation had not happened at all. Jace walked back into the room and I turned to him. He gave me a wide smile.

"I called Bastian and Lynne," he said with a sigh, "They'll be here in an hour. So, that means eight of us will know."

I nodded and took a deep breath as I finally began to relax because no matter what I faced, I wasn't alone now.

****

Lynne burst through the door with as much energy as ever. Even the wind seemed to react to her, following her into the room and whipping around the whole area before disappearing.

I watched her as she came fully inside the living room only stopping when she saw me standing beside the couch. A frown furrowed her brow as if she did not want to be in my presence.

"Hi," she said, taking two more steps and stopping. She shifted uncomfortably before walking into the center of the living room and looking at Catherine and then, Jace. It was obvious she was questioning the reason for this meeting, especially since I was in attendance.

Bastian followed, looking at me warily. I glanced at Catherine and sighed before rolling my eyes. I could not believe that Lynne had once loved me like a sister and Bastian had once cared enough to try to help me. Their coldness toward me hurt.

"Don't worry," I said, sarcastically, "I won't open a vein in front of you."

Lynne closed her eyes and when she opened them again she looked upset, "You don't know what that did to us," she said, through clenched teeth, "It was very selfish."

I pursed my lips and narrowed my eyes at her. Catherine stepped forward about to defend me but I held up my hand to stop her. She blinked and nodded her head.

"So, there's nothing I can say that will make you less angry with me?" I said, tilting my head to the side.

"No," Lynne said, crossing her arms over her chest. I shook my head at her stubbornness.

"Fine," I whispered and her eyes widened as I said a bit louder, "I'll show it to you."

I didn't give her time to protest. Instead, I blew

the light that allowed me to show my visions out towards her and Bastian. Lynne narrowed her eyes as the light traveled toward her. She would not have been able to escape it if she'd wanted to. Once my gift was in motion, it would not stop until it found the source I sent it too. Her face reddened as the light traveled up her nostrils and into her mind. She blinked and then, closed her eyes. When she opened them tears glowed within their depths.

She blinked again as the tears escaped from her eyes and traveled down her cheeks. Her mouth opened in an o of shock as the light dimmed. A moment of absolute silence passed before she looked at me again.

"Alex, why didn't you tell me?" She asked, placing her hands on her hips. A slight tremble shook her but she continued to look into my eyes.

"Because you wouldn't have listened," I said, tilting my head to the side, "You're a show me type of girl. So, I showed you."

Lynne blushed, "yeah…I can't deny that," she said as a sob escaped her throat, "Oh, Alex. I'm so sorry."

"Me too," Bastian said, quietly. I smiled at him. I had almost forgotten he was still in the room.

"You're forgiven," I said, pursing my lips, "You didn't know. But if you're still feeling guilty you can make amends. I need your help."

Bastian stepped forward and placed a large, thick file on the coffee table, "And you already have it."

"Is that the file on Jezebel?" I asked, narrowing my eyes at the thick folder. Maybe there was an answer to her destruction inside.

"It is," he said, raising his brows, "Jace asked me to bring it. I've been trying to find a way to defeat her for a while but it looks like you are the one with the answers or at least, you're beginning to be."

"I only know who helps the person to bring her down," I said, frowning, "I don't know who gives the final blow."

"You will," he said and then, handed me the folder, "And when you do, you'll have our help."

I nodded and then, breathed a sigh of relief. I had been alone for too long. To have people on my side felt good. I raised my chin. At least I was beginning to defeat Jezebel in this. She had wanted them to believe I was crazy. One by one, I was proving to them I wasn't. I was getting back what she had thought she'd destroyed. I was getting back my life.

****

I laid in my bed staring up at the ceiling. Shadows played across the walls as I sighed. Everything was coming together. Still, uneasiness slid down my spine as my phone began to buzz on the night table beside my bed.

I reached over and turned off the phone without looking and pushed the button to send the caller to voicemail. A ping sounded a few moments later alerting me to a new message.

I sighed as my eyes filled with tears. Slowly, a tear released it hold and fell down my cheek. I knew who had called…Ky. I swallowed hard as my phone began to buzz again.

I closed my eyes as guilt flooded my heart. Even though I knew I had to let him go, it was hard to ignore him but I couldn't risk hurting him or myself especially while I went up against Jezebel. The only way I could prevent harm to either of us was to gain some distance from him…but it didn't look like he was going to let me do that easily.

As the ping happened again, my heart clenched. I took a deep breath as I began to cry. These tears were for me because my breaking heart told me it was already too late to prevent my harm. I had fallen for him but couldn't be with him because I didn't need my gift to see that it would end badly for us. The evidence was with my relationship with Daniel. If I couldn't hold on to someone who had known me my whole life, how could I hold someone who barely knew me. Worse, I had a gut feeling I would hurt him. So, I had to push him away for his benefit. I was no good for him…I was no good for anyone to be in love with because even though I hadn't tried to kill myself, I knew that I was still broken.

Chapter Seven
Feelings

I had managed to avoid Ky for a little under a week. School had started for me again and though I had nearly ran into him a few times in the hall, I had managed to see him before he saw me. I was so distracted trying to avoid him that I barely realized the stares I received as I walked through the halls. It was only when a girl actually came up to me and called me a freak that I realized the open-mouthed stares and whispers as people gave me fearful looks. Their fear made me wonder if they thought I was going to curse them or something. That seemed ridiculous because if they were so worried they wouldn't dare talk about me in too loud whispers or stare too long.

Even though I had not noticed the stares or the

taunts until Thursday, I was still relieved when Friday came. Unfortunately, I would still have to avoid Ky. Over the week, he had called every ten minutes after school. His messages were heartbreaking and I had stopped listening to them. They made me want to answer. They made me want to give in even though it was not good for either of us.

He had called again as I exited the bus on Friday and I sent him to voice mail feeling my heart sink in my chest. I was alone as I walked to the door because my siblings had opted to ride with Jeremy while I wanted to be alone for a while.

I looked toward the porch and sighed. I felt the strange mixture of relief and disappointment flow through me. I frowned trying to push away the regret and walked toward the door.

My hand was on the door knob when I felt his presence. I closed my eyes at the electrical awareness that whipped through me.

"Are you avoiding me, Alex?" He asked. The hurt was clear in his voice. My heart nearly broke but I didn't turn.

"It's not good for us to be around each other," I whispered, gripping the doorknob.

I felt him step closer, "Why do you think that?" He asked as he stood right behind me. I didn't dare turn because he would be too close and that frightened me.

"I'll end up hurting you," I whispered though that wasn't the whole truth either. I was afraid he would end up hurting me too.

"Don't you think I should be the one to decide if it's too much?" He asked so close I could feel his breath across my neck. I suppressed a shiver and turned pressing my back against the door to create some distance from him.

Slowly, I looked up at him. My chest clinched as I saw the absolute fear in his beautiful eyes. I blinked back tears as I realized it was already too late for him too. He already cared too much. He stepped back and ran his hand through his dark hair and then looked back at me with such a look of desperation that I would do anything…anything to make it disappear.

"You're right," I whispered, "I shouldn't have chose for you. I'm sorry."

"Alex, I can't let you go," he said as a tear ran down his cheek, "I can't lose someone else. Please don't make me."

I stepped in front of him and hugged him as tightly as I could, "I won't," I cried into his chest.

"Please don't cry, Alex," He whispered, as he kissed the top of my head, "If you really don't want to be my friend anymore then I understand. Just don't cry."

"I want to be your friend," I whispered and I felt him relax as his arms encircled me, "I just don't want to hurt you but it seems I already have."

"You won't hurt me, Alex," he said, softly, "Well, you will if you leave but besides that, you won't."

I raised my head and looked up at him, "I won't leave again," I whispered.

He raised his hand and wiped the tears from my cheeks as he smiled, "Good."

A cough sounded from behind us and we jumped back away from each other and turned to find Daniel. I frowned as I saw his eyes darken as he looked from me to Ky.

"You two look cozy," he said.

I shifted uncomfortably, "What are you doing here, Daniel?" I asked, frowning.

"We have a meeting today," He said, glaring at me, "Remember?"

Ky grasped my arm and pulled me to him protectively, "Why are you being such a jerk? You're the one who broke up with her…for another girl. If anyone should be in a bad mood, it's Alex."

Daniel shifted, "You're right," he said and then, looked at me, "But maybe I still care about who she's around."

"Well, lucky for me, you don't get to choose," I said, straightening my spine and turning to open the door. I kept my other hand firmly in Ky's, "Now, you can stay out here until the others arrive or you can come in but if you do, I would prefer if you didn't speak to me."

I continued to pull Ky with me inside, leaving Daniel gaping behind us.

****

The meeting was uncomfortable but necessary.Thankfully, the files calmed my nerves as I read the translated information Bastian had found. What I did not want was to experience sympathy for Jezebel but as I read, I couldn't help but to feel sad for how she must have felt.

She had been an angel once. She had been appointed to protect humans and she had been good at her job. She had shown compassion and love. Unfortunately, that seemed to be what caused her downfall. Her ability to give absolute love. She had fallen in love with Asmodis and fell with him when he denied God. Though she had given up everything for him, Asmodis never loved her back. He had used her for his own gratification, causing her to become a lust demon. She never liked causing lust and chaos. She viewed it as a punishment. Her existence was pure hell.

I frowned as I put the papers down. I couldn't help the ache in my heart for her. Even after everything Asmodis had done, she still loved him and wanted to avenge him. It did not matter to Jezebel what his true feelings were.

I closed my eyes wishing I had never read the file. Instead, I wanted to pretend that she was purely evil but I couldn't. She had been an angel who had fallen with the one she loved. Yes, she had made a mistake for doing so. She had turned her back on God but I had made mistakes too. What had I once been willing to do for Daniel? I wouldn't have given my soul like she had but I had nearly given my life. Even as I sat within the same room with Daniel there was someone else who was beginning to grip my heart the same way he had…Ky. I shook my head but I was unable to shake the image of Jezebel as just a woman in love.

I was still deep in thought when everyone but my siblings left and my mother arrived. She frowned when she looked at me, taking in my mood.

"Are you okay?" She asked, tilting her head to the side as she studied me.

"A little confused," I said giving her a small smile and shrugging. She looked at me quizzically and I continued, "Someone I thought of as black-hearted, may not be. I guess I just got new insight to this person."

My mother smiled widely, "There are different layers to everyone," she said, "No one is purely bad and no one is purely good. It's something you should remember."

"I will, Mom," I said and then, motioned toward the sliding glass door leading to the deck, "For now, I just want some time to think."

My mother nodded her head, "Just make sure to come in soon," she said, "I don't like for you to be out there too late. I'm afraid something bad could happen and I wouldn't know."

"I will," I said with a crooked smile. If only she knew the things that had already happened, she'd never let us out of the house again.

"Okay," she said and then, patted my cheek, "Call for me if you need me."

"I will," I said as I pulled open the sliding glass doors and stepped outside.

My mother stood in the doorway for a few moments before turning and walking toward her bedroom, obviously satisfied nothing was going to happen. I crossed the deck to stand at the railing to look out over the back yard. Slowly, I smiled.

"I see everything hasn't changed," I heard Daniel behind me.

I stiffened as I turned with narrowed eyes. I looked toward the driveway seeing that his car was not there. He had used his gift to transport from one place to the other.

"No," I said, angrily, "You still have the creepy habit of sneaking up on people. You might want to get help for that. Most people call it stalking."

"I'm not stalking you," he said, frowning. His brown eyes darkened, "I just need to talk to you without everyone else around."

"Well get it over with so you can leave," I said and bit my tongue to keep from saying anything else.

"Alex, I'm trying to be nice," he said, "I still care about you."

I scoffed and shook my head, "Don't lie. If you cared about me, you would have at least waited two weeks to break it off with me. Don't pretend you didn't have a choice. You did and you didn't love me, nor did you care about my feelings at that time."

"Alex, I'm not lying," he said with tears welling in his eyes, "And I do care. It's why I'm here. I'm worried about you hanging out with Ky. I don't like him."

I laughed, "Really," I said, sarcastically, "I thought he was your best friend."

"He's not a good person for you to spend all of your time with," he said, quickly.

"Neither were you but I still did," I said, and then, shook my head ready to end this discussion, "I don't know why you are here, Daniel but who I hang out with is absolutely none of your business. Just like who you hang out with is none of mine."

I started to walk past him and he grabbed my arm. I jerked it away from him, "One more thing," I hissed, "You might want to remember a lot has changed in just a few months but my will to fight is a lot stronger. Frankly, I'm pissed at you so keep your hands off me."

Then, I walked through the door, sliding it closed. When I looked back outside, he was gone. Tears burned my eyes as anger burned through me. I groaned, wanting to scream in frustration. Instead, I grabbed my phone and walked back to my room with the intent to call Ky.

****

I felt better as I lay in my bed. Ky had laughed about Daniel's visit and I found myself laughing too. It had been ridiculous. I also ended the call with plans to go to a teen club in the neighboring town the next night to search for Jezebel. For once, I would not be stuck at home.

However, as I slept uneasiness crept over me. It took a moment to realize it was because I wasn't alone. Semerias had come to visit. I had blinked and opened my eyes to find him standing over me. I jumped disturbed.

"Can't you ever show up without scaring me?" I asked, looking up at him annoyed.

He frowned, "All I did was look at you."

"I know. It was creepy," I said, sitting up and looking toward Kelly's bed. She was still sound asleep. I looked back at him and he was frowning, puzzled.

"There are always angels looking at you," he said looking distressed.

"I can't see them," I said, rising from my bed.

He gave me a crooked grin, "They're still there."

I rolled my eyes, "What do you want, Semarias?"

"I wanted to check on your progress with Jezebel's final downfall," he said with raised brows.

"Shouldn't you know this?" I asked, frowning, "You *are* an angel."

"Angels aren't all-knowing," he said with raised brows, "We only know enough to do our missions. We learn everything the same way you do."

"No you don't," I smiled widely as I faced him, "You get your information from someone who is all-knowing."

He nodded, "So do you…even if it isn't directly," he said, "So, now will you answer my question."

I shrugged, "I only know pieces of what is going to happen when her downfall comes," I said, frowning, "I saw Catherine hindering her but she's not the one who brings her downfall and of course, Kelly pulls her out of the one she's possessed but I don't know who her host is. I only know she's female."

"It sounds like you've found a great deal," he said with a gentle smile.

"Then, why do I feel like a failure?" I asked with a sigh.

"Human nature is strange," he said and then, really looked at me, "Maybe it's because you are self-conscious right now. Everyone has judged you because of your looks and it's caused you to judge yourself. They don't have faith in you, so you've lost faith in yourself."

"How do you have faith in me?" I asked, tilting my head as I looked at him, "You don't really know me."

He frowned and then, nodded his head, "I see everything from inside of you," he said and shrugged, "I see determination, love and beauty. Your appearance means very little to me or any other angel."

"Sounds like I could be friends with them," I whispered.

He laughed, filling my room with it's clear, deep timbre, "I know I may seem cold and single-minded when it comes to my missions, but you do have a friend in me, Alex."

I smiled and he sighed, "I must go. I left the pit guarded by another angel. We have to make sure not to let anything else out."

My eyes widened, "Then, please get back to that pit,." I said, alarmed, "We don't need to fight another demon."

"Good-bye, Alex," He said, smiling, "And get some sleep."

I grinned, "As long as you stop staring at me while I'm sleeping."

"I can't promise that won't happen again," he said, "But not for the rest of the night."

I nodded and he was gone. I laid down in my bed and fell quickly into a dream.

Chapter Eight
Storms

Thunder roared outside as the dream came to me. I frowned as I looked around my bedroom. Slowly, I rose from my bed. Kelly still slept sound as I made my way to the door. The only odd thing that told me I stood within a dream was Leighton standing within the doorway.

"I see you're still dream jumping," I said with raised brows, "Though you chose to forget to do that while I was in the hospital."

"No, I didn't forget," he said, narrowing his brown eyes, "I didn't think you would want me to. Besides, Gloria thought it was better for you if I didn't."

"So, why are you here now?" I asked, looking at him for the first time in months. A lot had changed with him since I had been away. His wiry frame had become lean and muscular. He had grown taller. He had shaved his head, giving no evidence of his very curly brown hair. His eyes were still surrounded by wire frames but had become darker. Still, there was something proving him to be quiet and awkward.

He shifted as if uncomfortable, "We need to talk and I didn't want to do that in front of everyone else."

"Why do I hear that all of the time lately?" I asked, smiling.

"It's probably because everyone knows something doesn't feel right," he said, walking closer to me.

"Why do you say that?" I asked, narrowing my eyes.

"Because I've seen your dreams," he said, frowning, "And you've dreamed about the night you supposedly tried to kill yourself," he frowned as he tilted his head to study me, "You didn't do it, did you? It was Jezebel."

I stared at him for a few moments. He shifted as I nodded, "It was Jezebel," I said with a sigh, "But I couldn't tell anyone then. Some know now."

"Who else knows?" He asked, stepping fully into the room.

"Catherine, Jace, Lynne, Bastian, Micah, Ky and my brothers and sister," I said, frowning.

"When were you going to tell me?" he asked, looking hurt.

"When it was your time to know," I said, shrugging, "That seems to be now."

"So, will you tell me what's going on?" He asked, tilting his head, "I mean, will you tell me the rest of it?"

"I will but first, I need for you to cast anything out

of this dream that shouldn't be here," I said with raised brows, "And I also need for you to keep anything from coming in."

"I have already done that," he said, grinning, "I kind of figured you didn't want Jezebel here while I was talking to you."

"Thanks," I said, looking around the room relieved.

"So, what's really going on?" He asked, frowning.

"Well, you saw that Jezebel is the one who slit my wrists," I said wincing at the memory.

He nodded, "You dream about Jezebel's attack a lot," he said and then, shifted uneasily, "I am sorry I thought you tried to commit suicide. We *all* should have known better."

"I forgive you," I said, pinching the bridge of my nose before looking back at him, "Sometimes, it is hard to understand what is real and what is not. I can understand why everyone is confused."

"We don't deserve your understanding...especially Daniel," he said and then, wrinkled his nose in disgust, "Does he know?"

I shook my head, "No, he doesn't and he doesn't need to know right now."

"It was an asshole move he pulled," he said, narrowing his eyes.

"Yeah but he's pulled a lot of those lately," I said with a sad half-smile, "I'm getting used to it."

Leighton grinned, "I guess you would," he said and then, crossed the room and sat on a chair near my bed. I sat down on the edge of my bed facing him.

"So, what is the rest of it?" Leighton asked,

searching my face.

"Well, you know Jezebel is going to continue to attack me in any way she knows will hurt," I said, frowning, "Everyone is in danger but Daniel stands to lose his soul."

Leighton frowned and then, looked up at me in alarm, "So, she'll come after us to get to you?"

I nodded my head, "And since she believes I am the only reason Asmodis was sent back to hell and he was the one she loved, she'll go after Daniel because he has been my love since childhood."

"What about Ky?' Leighton asked and I threw back my head and groaned. I lowered my head and looked at him.

"She'll probably go after him next…especially since everyone insists I am dating him. She probably assumes that too."

"You're not dating him?" He asked, confused.

"No," I said, annoyed.

Leighton winced, "I'm sorry," he said with a shrug, "It just seemed like you were."

I shook my head and waved my hand in front of my face, "Anyway, I know someone from the Appointed is supposed to defeat her but I can't tell who. I can tell it's not Catherine and of course, Kelly pulls her out of the body she possesses before that but she's not the one who kills Jezebel either. Honestly, I don't see anything else. So, I don't know who lands the final blow."

"So, it's not Catherine or Kelly but they help," he said, "Maybe I can help figure out who does kill Jezebel."

"You can't," I said and then, narrowed my eyes,

88.

"Semerias told me *I* have to figure it out."

"Who's Semerias?" He asked, frowning.

"Oh…He's an angel," I said, shifting, "He is waiting at Jezebel's entrance point to make sure it's sealed when she's sent back. He can't seal it until we do our jobs."

Leighton's eyes widened, "Is there anything else?"

"Not really," I said with a shrug, "You're pretty much caught up."

"And why aren't you telling everyone yet?" He asked, frowning.

"It is mostly because I don't want Jezebel to realize Kelly and Catherine help," I said, looking into his eyes, "If I say anything about them and she hears, then, she will try to take them out. I can't allow that. Right now, she's still focused on me."

"You realize, you don't always have to be the sacrifice, Right?" he asked, looking into my eyes, worried, "Look what happened last time. You died."

"I remember," I whispered, "Probably better than you."

"I'm sure," he smiled, "Well, I better let you finish dreaming. There might be something important you need to be paying attention to."

"There probably is," I said, smiling as he faded, leaving me to dream my own dreams.

****

The club Ky took me to was called No Hearts Valentine's. I frowned at the name wondering how ironic it was that teenagers came there to find love. Still, as we walked in I understood why he thought Jezebel might show her face.

In every corner, there seemed to be people making out. On the dance floor, teenagers ground themselves against each other. Even the beat of the music was seductive. If Jezebel was going to show up anywhere, it would be within the club.

"Do you want to dance," Ky asked as I looked around again. I looked back at him and frowned. The dim glow cast shadows over his face, making him even more handsome.

I bit my lip and shifted uncomfortably, looking anywhere but at him. I saw that there were people who dressed like me but there were some of the other kids at school there too.   Still, I felt as if I belonged. I smiled as a band I recognized played over the loud speakers and thought of Everly. She would love it here.

Finally, I smiled up at Ky and nodded, "Let's dance."

He grabbed my hand and pulled me to the floor, pulling me into his arms as the slow song floated through the air. He pulled me close to him and I tensed.

"Don't worry," he whispered, "It's just a dance."

I blushed and rolled my eyes, "I know."

"Then, loosen up," he said with a grin and I nodded my head as I wrapped my arms around his neck. The music wrapped around us enveloping us and making it seem as if we were the only two in the room. After a while, I relaxed and rested my head on his shoulder, completely comfortable and at peace in his arms as we swayed to the music. I hadn't realized the music had ended until he pulled away. I looked up at him still caught in the magic of the song. He smiled crookedly as he cupped my cheek. I blinked, breaking the spell and backed away.

"Do you think Jezebel will really show up?" I asked, nervously.

"Alex," he whispered as if frustrated and then, shook his head, "Yes, I do."

I nodded and turned toward the tables. He followed me and stopped on the other side of the table I had chosen before sitting down. He looked around anxiously.

"I'm going to get us some drinks," he said, softly.

I smiled as I nodded at him, "Thanks."

He gave me another crooked grin and walked to the bar. I watched him for a few moments before turning my attention back to the dance floor. That's when I saw Daniel with Renee. They were kissing passionately. My breath caught in my throat as tears filled my eyes. I rose quickly not knowing what to do and before I realized it, I had run out the door. Ky yelled after me and then, I heard him running as he followed me into the back alley.

Thunder rumbled as Ky called for me again. I stopped walking, not facing him as the wind whipped around me. I took a few deep breaths before I turned to look at him.

"Alex, I'm sorry," he said as worry creased his brow.

I swallowed hard as the first drop of rain fell on my cheek. I raised my chin as I looked at him.

"You didn't know," I said as tears swam in my eyes.

The wind twirled around me as my hair blew back from my face. Thunder rumbled, getting closer and closer. Ky stepped toward me.

"Why do you want to be around me," I cried, feeling my heart break, "I'm nothing…I'm…broken."

Ky's eyes widened and shock crossed his face, "You aren't nothing."

A sob broke from my throat, "Yes, I am."

He shook his head as he crossed the distance to me and before I knew what had happened, he had pulled me to him. Tears fell down his face mingling with the rain that had begun to fall from the sky.

"You aren't nothing," he whispered, "Alex, you're everything to me. You are holding me together."

My eyes widened as he leaned in and pressed his lips to mine. I closed my eyes sensing his love for me and gave in, kissing him back. I knew without a doubt that I loved him too. He had found a way to heal me when my heart had been smashed. He found worth in me when everyone else seen me as worthless.

I reached up and grabbed his cheeks with both hands and poured everything into the kiss. Slowly, I traced his beautiful lips with my tongue. I felt his smile as he pulled away and caressed my cheek with the back of his hand. I sighed as I leaned into it.

"Alex, you have no idea how much I care for you," he whispered, "But if you would just forget what he did and be with me, I would never hurt you. Please give me a chance. Please."

I closed my eyes for a moment and then, nodded.

"Does that mean you'll give me a chance?" He asked warily.

I smiled and gave the answer that would give me a new start at my life, "Yes."

92.

Chapter Nine
Father's Daughter

I had been blissfully distracted by Ky for the weekend. Though we had decided to keep our relationship quiet until after Jezebel's defeat, we did not stay away from each other. Instead, I spent Sunday at his house playing music on his old record player.

Though we had sworn secrecy to everyone else, there was one person we did tell about our relationship...Micah. Thankfully, she was thrilled. Unfortunately, the others may not be as happy. Worse, I was afraid if they knew Jezebel would find out and use Ky for revenge against me. I couldn't allow that.

Still, I found it was already hard to go a Monday evening without him. Unfortunately, I had been summoned to a meeting with Bastian and Lynne and would have to endure it because no one else was allowed.

So, I sat on my couch beside Lynne with Bastian pacing in front of us gripping a file folder to his chest. Lynne bit her lip and shifted every few seconds. I frowned at their strange behavior because I knew something was going on and they didn't know how to tell me. I narrowed my eyes at them, suspiciously.

"So, why are you so nervous?" I asked looking at each of them before staring pointedly at the file clutched to Bastian's chest, "What's in that file that's making you act so strange?"

Bastian stopped pacing and glanced at me warily before pulling the file away from his chest and looking at it as if he would rather burn it than show me its contents. I raised an eyebrow at him. Whatever the file contained must be something horrible to upset him so much. Slowly, his eyes met mine.

"Before I give this to you, I want you to know that I had no knowledge of what's in this file," He said, looking troubled, "However, since it has something to do with you, I thought you should know."

I frowned, "What are you talking about?" I asked, looking at the file again as a knot settle in my stomach. Every time a secret had been kept from me it had been life threatening. I looked up into Bastian's face feeling panic creep up my spine, "What's in that file, Bastian?"

Bastian shifted and then, took a deep breath, "This file contains information about your father," he said, handing me the folder.

I blinked, surprised as I reached forward and took the file, "Why would there be a file on my father?"

"I think you should read it and see for yourself," he said, looking worried as I glanced down at it.

Slowly, I opened it, finding a picture of my father when he was around twelve years old. I looked up at Bastian one more time and then, scanned the material. Shock raced through me and I looked up at Bastian with wide eyes, "Could this be true?"

Bastian swallowed, "It *is* true," he whispered, "I checked it out. I'm so sorry, Alex."

"Reverend Boothe kept this from me?" I asked as tears burned my eyes. Betrayal and anger swept through me.

"Yes," Bastian said, softly, "But you have to remember my uncle always did things for a reason. Please don't be upset with him yet. Talk to your dad and find out what happened. You do know where he is, don't you?"

I nodded, "He moved back to Barrington during my stay at the hospital. I haven't seen him yet...but I think a visit is due."

Bastian nodded, "Do you need a ride?"

I nodded my head, feeling more angry and confused than I ever had.

****

As we drove up to my father's house, I felt every sadness he had ever given me. My heart broke as I remembered how he had looked passed out after a drinking binge or red-eyed after getting high. Worse, I remembered the times he ignored me. Those times had hurt worse than any others.

I swallowed pushing those memories away as his house became visible in the distance. Again, worry clenched my stomach as I stared at the house, realizing my father hadn't wanted to see me. He hadn't even invited me there since his return. Tears stung my eyes as hurt hammered through my heart.

I closed my eyes and took a deep breath as the car stopped and I reluctantly got out. I stared up at the house painted a light yellow with a small porch on the front. I stopped walking only when I saw my seven-year old sister, Ariel sitting on the porch steps.

She was a beautiful little girl with strawberry blonde curls and large hazel eyes. She was also the reason I had lived with my father for so long. I had taken care of her and had suffered a fair amount of guilt when I left. I smiled as I took in her face. Out of all of the darkness that had happened while living with my father, she had been the light.

Slowly, she raised her head and looked at me quizzically, taking in my appearance. I realized she didn't recognize me so I stepped closer until her eyes lit up. She rose quickly and ran to me, hugging me around my waist.

"Alex, you're back!" she said, happily. My heart clenched as I pulled her to me.

"Of course, I am," I said, hugging her tightly to me. My eyes narrowed. Jezebel had taken me away from my little sister too. It was another thing that helped me want her back where she belonged...in hell.

"I've missed you so much," she said, happily.

"I've missed you too," I whispered, feeling tears rise in my eyes. Slowly, I looked around, "Is your mom here?"

Silence greeted me and I looked at her, silently praying that my stepmother was not home. Felicia had never really welcomed me in her house. Slowly, Ariel shook her head.

"No, she went to the doctor," she said, frowning, "She's been throwing up a lot."

I bit my lip only wondering for a moment if it was something serious before pushing the thought away. I had other things to worry about.

"Where's Daddy?" I asked, frowning.

She pointed toward the house, "He's asleep," she said and then, pouted, "He told me to play out here until mom got home."

I nodded as the familiar anger returned. Again, Ariel was left by herself. I worried about her safety. I pressed my lips together and looked at Lynne and Bastian who nodded in sync and then, knelt to look at Ariel.

"These are my friends, Lynne and Bastian," I said, softly, "They wanted to play outside and I told them they had to meet you because you are the best person to play with in the entire world. Do you mind getting to know them while I talk to Daddy?"

She looked at them shyly, "Yeah, I'll stay with them," she said, smiling up at Lynne, "Maybe we can play hide and seek."

"You bet we can," Lynne said, feigning excitement, "It's one of my favorite games."

"Mine too," Ariel said, excited.

"I'll be back out in a few minutes," I said and she nodded her head vigorously.

I lost my smile as I walked to the house, determined to get answers. I didn't knock before I entered. My father probably wouldn't have heard me if I had. I stood just inside the door finding him in his favorite chair with a plate beside him resting precariously on the arm. A beer was gripped in his hand and his eyes were closed.

"Daddy!" I called as frustration slid up my spine and he moaned, "Daddy!" I screamed again.

Finally, he opened his glazed blue eyes. He blinked up at me, jumping when he finally recognized me. He blinked a few more times, "Alex?"

"Yeah, Daddy," I said, standing over him, "It's me."

"What are you doing here?" He asked, frowning as he sat up.

"I need to talk to you," I said, narrowing my eyes "I found out some things about you that affect me. I need for you to tell me the truth for once."

He blinked his eyes and then ran his hand over them before looking at me again, "I don't think you have the right to ask me anything," He said, leaning up, "You left, remember."

"You told me you understood," I said with narrowed eyes, "I never wanted to quit speaking to you. You decided that all on your own."

"You abandoned me," he said, narrowing his eyes, "You decided you didn't want to be around me anymore."

"You did something worse, Daddy," I said, looking into his eyes. Silence hung between us thick and suffocating.

"What are you talking about, Alex?" He asked warily straightening in his chair.

"The Appointed, Daddy…Do you know of them?" I asked, watching as his eyes widen.

"Where did you find out about them?" He asked, looking at me carefully.

"I *am* one of them," I said through my teeth, "I have the gift you gave up."

"What?" He asked in shock and then, shook his head, "You're lying."

"No, I'm not," I said, narrowing my eyes, "Who did you think your gift would be given to when you refused to use it?"

He looked at me warily, "You don't know everything."

"What do I not know, Daddy?" I asked, feeling my heart break as I looked at him, "Tell me."

He nodded and then, rubbed his hand down his face. When he looked at me his eyes were full of remorse.

"I had more than one gift," he said and my eyes widened, wondering if that could be true, "I couldn't handle all of them. God must have saw the trouble I was having and sent an angel…Semerias," he said and my eyes widened at the name, "He told me I could release one gift so I could handle the rest. He did warn me it would go to someone else. I didn't think about who the gift would go to until after I let it go. When I did think about it, the guilt was too much because I suspected who would have it. I guess I was right."

"How many gifts do you have?" I asked, narrowing my eyes.

"Three more," he said, frowning, "It was the first time someone had been given more than one gift. I guess the Appointed have habits of marrying each other."

"And you had four gifts," I said, shaking my head,

"How did you handle it? How do you handle having three now?"

"They're not so bad," he said with a shrug, "It's the guilt of who they go to if I let them go. Seeing the future went to you. The others will go to my other children when I die," he said as a tear fell down his cheek, "I've already made the mistake of giving one to you. I don't want to do that willingly again."

I frowned as I thought of my siblings. Through my father, I had a brother, Matt and of course, Ariel. So, they would most likely take two of his gifts when he passed. The other one was in limbo.

"What are the gifts?" I asked, shifting disturbed.

"I can create wind with my breath," he said, shrugging, "I can see ghosts and I can find things that are missing. It's like there's a map to it in my head."

"So, those gifts will go to Ariel and Matt?" I asked, frowning.

He nodded, "And the son or daughter I have on the way," he whispered.

I closed my eyes as I realized why Felicia was sick. I felt my heart squeeze in my chest. I would have another brother or sister, "Felicia's pregnant?"

My father nodded, "I had four gifts and will have four children," he said and nodded as if deciding what to say next, "Something you need to remember, everything comes full circle," he said, "I am convinced I was appointed with these gifts to give them to my children. All of you, will be part of a group who will do something great…greater than I ever could."

"Daddy, you could have done something great with your gifts," I said, taking a deep breath, "You still

100.
can."

He shook his head, "Look at me," he said, motioning to himself, "Alex, I'm too old and sick. The only thing I can do now is try to hold on to the gifts as long as I can. I can't deal with the guilt of giving your siblings these powers."

I nodded, seeing him clearly for the first time. He was frightened for us…for his children. For the first time, I truly felt his love. I leaned down and hugged him, holding onto my father and wishing I knew how to help him.

Chapter Ten
Promises

When I left my father, I left him on better terms
than I had arrived. Though a deep sadness resonated
within me, I understood him better than ever. On some
level, I realized every one of his problems led back to
guilt over releasing one of his powers and his worry that
it had gone to me. Now that his worst fear was realized, I
wondered if his problems would become worse.

Truthfully, I worried about him. He was in
constant fear and it would only rise to greater and greater
intensity, especially since he worried he would release
his gift to his newborn child. The thought made me
tremble and for a moment I realized how intense his fear
was.

As I sat in the back seat of the car, I was free to

think. It was only when we were almost to my house, I noticed how quiet everyone was. Surprisingly, even Lynne sat mutely staring out the window of the front passenger window. I tilted my head as I studied her. She was never quiet. I glanced at Bastian unnerved but he only continued to glimpse at me in the rearview mirror. It seemed there was something he wanted to say but had not gotten the nerve yet.

We were in the living room before Bastian turned to me. A note of unease colored his words, "Your father really was one of us?" He asked, shifting his eyes from me to Lynne.

I nodded, "He kind of still is," I whispered, "He was the first Appointed to have multiple gifts. He did give one away and that's the one I have. He still has three left. I don't think he'll ever use them to help us but since he still has them, he's still technically one of the Appointed."

"He's not the first to have multiple gifts. You can blow out your memories to us," Bastian said, frowning, "And Sarah not only talks to animals but can shift into them."

I shook my head, "Those are extensions to our existing gifts," I said, frowning, "Each of my father's gifts are unique. He can create wind with his breath, find missing things and see ghosts. All of them are completely different. They can't be used together like my gifts or Sarah's."

"How was he able to give his gift to you?" He asked and then, threw his hands up, "As far as I knew, the Appointed only received gifts when another

Appointed died."

"I know that rule well," I said thinking of Micah, "But God sent the angel, Semerias to give my dad the choice."

Bastian frowned and his face reddened, "Uncle Asa knew," he said, shaking his head, "That means..."

I narrowed my eyes, "Drake, Gloria and Micah knew."

Bastian nodded his head as my heart dropped. They had allowed me to be angry with my father by keeping secrets. I had to find out why.

****

Bastian and Lynne left and I looked around my living room trying to decide what to do. Gloria and Drake were aware of my father's involvement in the appointed but they had not really spoken to me since my return from the hospital. However, Micah also knew and somehow I was sure she would tell me the truth.

My decision made, I pulled my cellphone from my pocket and dialed Ky. He could detect something wrong with my voice as soon as he answered the phone. When I told him I wanted to see his mother, he agreed to come get me.

Fifteen minutes later, I was in the front passenger seat of his car with my hand placed in his. I bit my bottom lip as we headed toward his house, worrying about how to ask Micah about my father. Ky turned to me and frowned.

"Okay...What's wrong?" He asked, quirking one eyebrow at me.

I blushed and took a deep breath, "I found out

something about my dad today and your mom knows about it."

He frowned, suddenly protective, "It won't upset her, will it?"

"I don't really see why she would be upset," I said, tilting my head. I sighed and began to explain, "My dad was one of the Appointed. Reverend Boothe, Gloria, Drake and Micah kept that from me. I want to know why they didn't tell me."

"Are you mad?" He asked, frowning.

"I'm upset they didn't tell me but I'm not horribly mad. I feel like there was a reason...a good one," I said and then, shrugged, "Besides, it doesn't do well to keep secrets like that in the Appointed. Maybe I just want to make sure that's all. I don't need to be surprised by anything else right now."

"I'm sure mom will understand that," he said, giving me a lopsided smile, "Regardless, she needs to tell you. She doesn't need a secret like that stressing her out."

I nodded as we pulled into the driveway of Micah's plantation style home. It was always hard for me to imagine Ky living in such a place. It didn't seem his style.

Ky got out and closed his door before walking around to the passenger side door and opening it. He held out his hand.

"We're on safe ground," he said, smiling widely, "So, I get to hold your hand."

I grinned as I put my hand in his and walked into the house. Once inside, I looked around the familiar living room and smiled. It was decorated in warm blues and light wood. It was bright and airy. I sighed suddenly content. There was something about the room which reminded me of the sitting rooms of Victorian women but I couldn't quite put my finger on what that was.

As I scanned the room again, I found Ky's twelve year old sister, Aubrey. sitting on the sofa reading a book. She looked up with wide surprised eyes the same color as Ky's when she realized she wasn't alone. She looked at our clasped hands and grinned.

"Where's mom?" Ky asked, smiling at his little sister.

"She's upstairs," she said and then, raised her brow as she looked at me, "She must have been expecting you because she wanted to talk to you when you got here."

I frowned as I realized Bastian or Lynne must have called to warn Micah that I knew about my father. I couldn't be angry with them about that. They were just trying to protect her.

Ky nodded and shrugged before he pulled me up the long curving stairwell. I looked back and waved at Aubrey when we reached the top. She waved back with a giggle.

We reached the first room at the top of the stairs and Ky knocked. I heard Micah's weak voice through the door bidding us to come in. *How sick had she become in just two weeks?* Suddenly, I dreaded seeing her.

Ky turned the knob and opened the door. I followed him into the room. Micah sat in the middle of a large canopy bed surrounded by snow-white netting. The fabric was pulled back and tied to the posts so I could see her lying within the bed. She was thinner than she had been even two weeks before. Her skin looked pale but had a bruised quality within her cheeks and beneath her eyes. When she looked at me, I saw the brown irises of her eyes had turned a brownish red and blood vessels had broken around them. My heart lurched and I had an extreme urge to run.

"Alex," Micah said, weakly, stopping my thoughts from becoming a reality. I raised my chin and blinked to fight back tears of grief and shame.

I opened my mouth to speak but found I had to force the words past my lips, "Hello, Micah," I whispered.

"Bastian called," She said, slowly sitting up in the bed. She struggled with the pillows until Ky stepped forward and helped to make her comfortable. Finally, she looked at me again, "He told me you knew about Ryan."

"I found out today," I said, nodding my head. A tear fell down my cheek as I smiled, "My dad does love me."

"Yes, he does," she said, tilting her head, "I'm sorry you ever doubted it."

"Why didn't you tell me?" I asked, quietly.

She smiled, "Because I was trying to protect him," she pursed her lips and sighed as she explained, "There's always been something…broken about your dad. I was afraid if I told you, you would confront him and confirm you were the one who had inherited his gift. I didn't think he could handle it."

"You were afraid of what it would do to him," I confirmed and she nodded her head.

She bit her lip as she blinked a tear from her eye. A look of pure remorse crossed her face as she gazed into my eyes, "He started taking painkillers and began drinking soon after giving up one of his gifts," she said and then, looked at me sadly, "I don't think he was aware of the consequences. I don't think Semerias explained that to him."

I narrowed my eyes, "I have met Semerias," I said and her eyes widened in shock, "He visits me. He will visit me again and I'll ask him what happened with my father."

She frowned, "There must be something with your bloodline," she said, "Angels tend to visit people from it. They visited Adele too. I guess you didn't know she was your great Aunt," She said, and I frowned. Adele was the woman who had my gift before my father. I looked up at Micah as she continued to speak, "They've never visited the rest of us."

I frowned and pursed my lips, "Maybe I need to ask him about that too."

"You should," Micah said, sleepily. Guilt pierced me as I saw how tired she was.

"I will, but you should rest," I said, taking her hand and squeezing it slightly.

"I'm sorry," she said, sighing heavily, "I seem to tire more as I get closer to…"

"I understand," I cut in not wanting her to finish the rest of that dreadful sentence, "Thank you for telling me the truth Micah."

108.

  "You're welcome," she whispered as Ky helped her lie down, "Just try to fix things with your dad now. Time is too precious and before you know it, it's gone."

  I opened my mouth to reply but she had already closed her eyes in sleep. My heart ached as I looked at Ky who was trying not to cry. I swallowed over the lump in my throat, knowing that every moment spent with Micah was precious because too soon she would be gone.

Chapter Eleven
Confrontations and Realizations

I looked out of the windshield in silence as Ky drove back to my house. An emergency meeting had been called and we were required to attend. I assumed this had something to do with my dad and I couldn't help but think of everything that had happened.

Everything raced through my mind in rapid speed not allowing me to focus on one subject too long before flitting to the next but one theme came up quite a bit...Micah.

I looked at Ky. I couldn't imagine losing my mother. The thought terrified me and made me want to find my mom and hold her close. It was quickly becoming my new worst fear. It was strange how until recently she had been nearly invincible in my mind. Now, I was terrified I was going to lose her. My heart ached for Ky because he would lose his mother. It was his reality and I found that there was nothing I could say to make him feel better.

"Alex," He whispered when the silence stretched too long, "I know why you're quiet. You shouldn't be. I need for you to help me."

"How?" I asked, fighting the sob that fought to escape my throat, "You're mother is sick. I can't find a way to save her when there isn't one."

He smiled and somehow, it seemed genuine even with all of the heartache surrounding him, "Just do what you've always done. Be here with me. Don't let me be alone."

"It doesn't seem like I'm doing very much," I said, softly. He met my eyes and through the sadness, I could see peace.

"You're doing plenty. At least, you being here means a lot to me," he said and gave my hand a gentle squeeze before turning into my driveway. I blinked in surprise. I hadn't even realized we had arrived at my house.

"Put on a smile," he said, sadly, "We have to face the others and we don't want them to worry."

I frowned, "I wonder how many times you've hid your pain for me."

He smiled, crookedly, "Most of the time I don't have to fake a smile for you," He gave me a full grin, "You make me laugh."

"Because I'm so funny looking," I said, narrowing my eyes at him.

He shook his head and laughed, "No, you're beautiful. You make me laugh because I'm happy."

I blushed and smiled, shyly, "I'm glad I can make you happy."

He released my hand, raising it in front of me about to caress my cheek when a knock came to the window. He quickly lowered his hand. We both turned to see that Lynne stood outside with an uncharacteristic frown on her face.

He rolled down his window and she stuck her head through and looked from me to Ky.

"We have a *huge* problem," she said, clearly upset.

I opened my door and got out. Lynne raised up and backed away from the car, allowing Ky to open his door.

I faced her, confused, "What's wrong?"

"Daniel brought Renee to the meeting," she said, clearly panicked.

My eyes widened and I looked at Ky, alarmed. I turned back to Lynne as anger flooded through me, "Does she know?"

Lynne's face reddened further, "Yeah," she said in a high-pitched voice, "He told her all of our gifts. He told her *everything*."

I inhaled, sharply, feeling the heat flood my face as I walked past Lynne and Ky. All I thought of was getting to Daniel and possibly killing him. He had just put everyone in danger.

I walked around the corner of my house to find everyone surrounding him. Ky and Lynne screamed my name as I walked through the crowd and landed a hard, loud blow across Daniel's cheek. He raised his hand caressing the red skin and looked at me stunned.

"Alex...damn it!" He screamed into my face.

"How dare you put all of us in danger!" I screamed, "What's wrong with you?"

"I didn't put us all in danger," he said, frowning,

"She's not going to tell anyone."

"How do you know that, Daniel?" I scoffed, "You've known her for a second and you've told her everything. I knew you were a jerk but I didn't realize you were a *dumbass*."

"Don't call me stupid," he said, angry again.

"Fine I'll call you selfish and self-centered," I said, raising my chin, "You told secrets that weren't yours to tell and you hurt everyone else because you couldn't keep your mouth shut!"

"I'm not trying to hurt anyone," he said, frowning, "Besides, she's not going to tell anyone."

"Good because if she's does, I'll beat the hell out of her," I said, narrowing my eyes.

"Why?" He asked, crossing his arms and smirking, "Because your jealous?"

I clenched my fists as my nostrils flared, "No, I'm not jealous. I just care more about our friends than you do."

Then, I turned and walked through the door of my house. I heard everyone else as they began yelling at Daniel again. I closed my eyes, wondering what was wrong with him.

****

I stood out on the deck trying to calm down. Even though I was forcing air through my lungs, my breaths were coming too quickly, causing me to feel dizzy. I was so angry I was shaking. I could not believe Daniel had told Renee about the Appointed. Worse, I couldn't understand why he had thought the reason for my anger was jealousy. I punched the railing, wincing when the rings I wore dug into the flesh of my fingers and palms.

"So, you *were* his girlfriend?" I heard Renee say, stopping me from hitting the deck again.

I turned to find her standing outside the sliding glass door. Her perfectly arched eyebrows were raised over her pretty brown eyes. Amusement crossed her face.

Slowly, I nodded my head, "I was," I said, frowning, "He cheated on me…with you."

No apology came from her lips. Instead, she smiled widely, "Well, I think he traded up. He didn't need to be with someone like you."

My mouth opened in shock, "What do you mean…someone like me?"

"Someone damaged," she said and smiled, "Someone who would bring him down with her….Someone who would destroy him."

I narrowed my eyes, confused, "You sound happy that he hurt me."

She walked across the deck to stand in front of me and shrugged, "I am happy about it," she grinned as she leaned closer and whispered, "Haven't you learned. Anything that gives you pain, makes me happy, Alex."

I inhaled sharply as she backed away, "Jezebel?"

She raised a brow and blinked twice, "Who's Jezebel?"

I opened my mouth to reply but Ky stepped through the door. He looked from me to Renee and frowned, "Is everything okay?"

"Yes," Renee said in a sugary sweet voice as she walked past Ky, clearly checking him out before entering the house. My eyes widened.

"Alex, what's wrong?" He asked grabbing my

shoulders and searching my face.

I took a deep breath and looked into his eyes, "I think I just found Jezebel's host," I said as anger flooded me, "I just have to prove it."

Chapter Twelve
When the Reaper Comes

The meeting ended very soon after it began. Everyone began to leave shortly after Daniel stormed away with Renee by his side. Sadly, Ky left also after a call from his dad to come home. When he received the call, I could tell that Micah wasn't feeling well. He had ducked his head as he spoke but I hadn't missed the tears shining in his eyes. I watched him leave with worry twisting in my gut.

Afterwards, Lynne and Bastian followed me as I walked up the steep steps to the deck.

"Micah isn't doing so well, is she?" Lynne asked. I faced her when I stood beside the railing and winced at the worry on her face. Micah was more than just one of the Appointed for her. She was her aunt.

"No, she isn't," I said, softly, watching as tears

filled her eyes.

"Do you think I need to go see her?" She asked, shifting. I smiled softly at her.

"You do," I whispered and she closed her eyes, releasing the tears that had been resting in them. Slowly, she nodded as she looked at Bastian silently pleading with him to take her to see her aunt.

"I'll take you," He said, softly.

"Before you go, I need to tell you something," I said, shifting uneasily before sighing heavily, "Believe me when I say that I know it's bad timing to bring this up but I'll need to meet you after school tomorrow because I think I might know who Jezebel is."

Bastian frowned and then, nodded at me, "We'll meet you tomorrow."

I nodded as Lynne walked across the deck and hugged me. Then, she was gone with Bastian following her down the deck stairs.

My brothers had left soon after Lynne and Bastian drove away. Kelly had started dance classes again. So, my mother had taken her to the placement auditions.

I was alone for the first time since leaving the Running Rivers and I didn't like it. I stayed out on the deck because somehow, it had always felt safer there. The house was too quiet to stay inside. For once, the deck only offered minimal solace.

"Alex," I heard Jenna say softly but it still caused me to leap in the air. I turned to find her smiling innocently. She blushed apologetic and even then she reminded me of an angel with golden hair and light eyes.

"I didn't mean to scare you," she whispered in a quiet voice.

"It's okay," I said, tilting my head confused, "I thought Clyde had given you a ride home."

She shook her head, "Leighton did, but I asked him to bring me back."

I tilted my head, surprised, "Why did you do that?" I asked, leaning back against the railing to the deck.

"Because of your aura," she said, frowning, "It doesn't make sense. Your aura shows your sense of survival is strong but you tried to kill yourself. When I asked Leighton about it, he wouldn't tell me anything. So, I asked to be brought back here."

I nodded and then, looked toward Leighton who had finally reached the top of the deck stairs, "See what I mean by I will tell people when it's their time to know?" I asked and he nodded his head.

I turned back to Jenna and smiled kindly, "Don't worry," I said, softly, "Your gift hasn't gone crazy. It's telling you the truth."

"But...how?" She asked, confused.

"Because I didn't try to kill myself," I said, raising my brows and waiting, "Jezebel attacked me."

"Jezebel slit your wrists," she said, frowning.

I nodded, "Why everyone was so willing to believe I had, I will never know. I would never try to take my life."

"Why didn't you tell us?" She asked frowning.

"Would you have believed me?" I asked and she shook her head shamefully. I shrugged as I continued, "It's okay. I guess I would have questioned it too," I studied her for a moment and then pursed my lips as I began to wonder if she saw more, " I do have to ask you something and it's important even if it doesn't seem that

118.
way."

"What is it?" She asked, frowning.

"You saw the truth when you looked at me. What did you see when you looked at Renee?" I asked, hoping that her ability would give me an absolute answer.

Jenna frowned and pursed her lips, "I haven't seen her."

"How is that possible when she was here today?" I asked, frowning as disappointment slammed through me, "I mean everyone else saw her. I know Lynne did. So did Ky and obviously Daniel."

"I saw her too," Leighton said, frowning, "Why are you asking about her aura."

"Because she said something that reminded me of Jezebel. She said, anything that gives me pain, makes her happy. Jezebel feels the same way because she thinks I killed Asmodis. She wants my pain," I said, watching as their eyes widened.

"You think Renee is possessed by Jezebel?" Jenna asked, frowning.

I took a deep breath, knowing they may not believe me, "Yeah," I whispered, "I do."

"If she is, Daniel is in trouble," Leighton said, looking terrified. I breathed a sigh of relief as I looked at him. He believed me and when I looked at Jenna, I knew she did too.

"What can we do about Daniel?" Jenna asked, shaking her head, "He's totally enthralled with her."

"Daniel made his choice," I said, feeling my heart sink, "He won't listen to any of us when it comes to her. He already told her all of our secrets. That proves he's more loyal to her than us."

"Yeah," Leighton whispered, "He's not going to listen."

"You've seen my dreams," I said, smiling sadly at Leighton, "You should tell Jenna what else is going on and we should do exactly as I've seen so far. It's the only way to save him."

"Okay," He said with a heavy sigh, "You know this is seriously messed up."

"Yeah," I said, closing my eyes for a moment. When I looked back at him a single tear fell down my cheek, "But be prepared. It will get much, much worse before it gets better."

Jenna and Leighton looked at me with terror clear on their faces. The problem was I couldn't comfort them at all.

****

I laid on my bed trying to sleep but every noise seemed magnified. Honestly, I didn't think sleep would come to me anyway. Everything that had happened raced through my mind, keeping my body from calming enough for even a daydream.

I grabbed my pillow and threw it over my face, blocking out the light. Even that didn't help and I found myself placing it back behind my head only a few minutes later.

Kelly's soft breath sounded throughout the room, taunting me that she could sleep and I couldn't. My eyes narrowed as I stared up at the ceiling knowing the reason for my unrest. I was hoping Semerias would show up so I could talk to him about my dad.

Finally, I parted my lips and whispered his name, hoping he would hear me. After a moment, the room became extremely quiet and then, I saw him standing at the end of my bed.

He raised an eyebrow and gave me a crooked grin, "You called?"

"I needed to talk to you," I said, frowning as I sat up. He pursed his lips as he looked at me warily. I licked my lips and whispered, "I found out about my dad."

He frowned as he lowered his wings into slits in his back, making him seem like a normal man. Slowly, he sat on my bed and faced me, "You know about your father giving away his gift?"

I nodded, "I also know it came to me," I said, feeling my eyes sting with tears, "I know about his guilt."

Semerias watched me, carefully choosing his next words. He reached forward and wiped away a tear that had fallen down my cheek, "What do you want to know?"

"Why did you offer my dad a choice to rid himself of one of his gifts?" I asked, frowning, "You had to know how much guilt he would feel."

"I didn't know," he said, sadly, "I told you, I'm not all-knowing."

"But you knew he was that type of person," I said as the tears nearly choked me. Semerias looked at me pained.

"He used to be different," he said almost in a whisper, "He was young and like most young people, he didn't think of the consequences. Besides, he was tortured. Having all of the gifts was hard on him. He couldn't deal with it."

"So, you felt bad for him?" I asked, raising my

eyebrows, "Is that why you gave him a choice?"

"I was told to," he said, biting his bottom lip, "Then, I was told to watch you. I'm not only a warrior of God, I am one of your guardian angels."

"You were appointed to me when I received my gift?" I asked, frowning.

He shrugged and then, nodded, "I had asked to be appointed to you at birth but was denied until you received your gift," he said.

"Why did you want to be appointed to me?" I asked, looking into his eyes.

"I saw what you would become when I touched you," he said, shrugging, "When that happens to an angel, an instinct to protect is there."

"So, I'm like your kid?" I grinned because he didn't seem much older than me.

Semerias gave a short laugh, "More like a soul mate."

I raised my eyebrow. I did not need an angel in love with me too.

He grinned, "It's not like that," he said, frowning, "Just the instinct is."

"So, you'd protect me like my true love?" I asked, grinning.

"That's exactly what I'm saying," he said.

"You know Asmodis killed me about eight months ago," I said with raised brows, "You didn't keep that from happening."

"It was supposed to happen," he said, shaking his head, "I didn't like it but I was told not to intervene. I didn't because I was promised, you would live again."

"Well, it's relieving to realize, you'll let me die if

you're told to," I said, rolling my eyes.

"Death doesn't hold the same meaning for angels as it does for humans," he said, blinking a couple of times, "To us, you'll just wake again in our world, which is a better place anyway. You would be with us and we wouldn't have to worry about your safety anymore. We would be happy. So would you."

I nodded as I truly understood. Slowly, I looked back at him, "There is something my dad said that's bothering me."

"That doesn't surprise me," Semerias said with a frown creasing his brow, "He worries me often."

I bit my lip and nodded, "He said, he thinks he got all those gifts just to pass down to his children," I said and shrugged, "He thinks that we were meant to do something great."

Semerias smiled sadly, "Your dad has always failed to see his importance. Unfortunately, you have inherited that trait. Your father still has his gifts for a reason. He needs to make a choice as to what to do."

"So, daddy has something else to do besides giving his children the gifts?" I asked, frowning.

"Yes, just like you, I am positive he will do it," he shrugged, "You both try to do right."

I rolled my eyes, "Yes, we do try."

"Just remember no human and no angel is perfect," he said with a sigh, "Only God is."

I nodded my head, "I'll keep that in mind," I looked into his eyes, "Can I ask you something else?"

He looked troubled but nodded, "You can ask me anything."

"Is there a reason why angels seem to come to my

family?" I asked, pursing my lips.

He rubbed his chin thinking, "Maybe it's because you each have sacrificed things for others. Sacrifice tends to open people's eyes."

I nodded, "I guess that makes sense."

He smiled and caressed my cheek before leaning forward to kiss my forehead. I frowned as heat spread across my skin. When he leaned back he smiled.

"You have a busy day tomorrow," he said, rising, "Your friend, Lynne, couldn't keep the secret anymore. She told her parents but don't hold it against her. She's had a hard day after seeing Micah."

"I knew she would eventually tell them," I said and then, sighed, "Your right though, it will be a long day tomorrow because Clyde will be coming to visit me too."

"He's a good man," Semerias said, softly.

"Yes, but he will be hurt that I didn't tell him," I said, feeling my heart sink. Somehow, hurting Clyde's feelings felt the same as if I had hurt one of my siblings.

"He'll understand after you explain," he said, softly, "Now, go to sleep. You'll need your strength. I'll see you again tomorrow."

I nodded and laid down, immediately falling to sleep and directly into a dream.

Chapter Thirteen
A Time for all things

As soon as I walked into school the next morning, Sarah grabbed me by the hand. My eyes widened in surprise. She hadn't spoken to me since my return from Running Rivers. Still, she seemed determined to speak to me as she pulled me through the school to the empty gym. Her grip was surprisingly firm. There was no way I would be able to jerk my hand from hers.

"What the hell, Sarah?" I asked, frowning as her hand tightened further, causing me to wince in pain, "I'll walk where you want me to. Let go!"

Slowly, she released me and turned, narrowing her blue eyes. Her brown hair was pulled into a high pony tail and her hands rested on her small hips. Honestly, she looked more like a cheerleader than a member of the Appointed but she was a member....one who could shape-shift into any animal she wanted. She was also able to speak to them in any form. As she faced me, she reminded me of a tigress and I was well aware she could change into one and attack me.

"What's going on?" She asked when she was sure we stood in the gym alone.

"What do you mean?" I asked, feigning ignorance.

She narrowed her eyes, "Fine. I'll go through the list."

I raised my eyebrows and smiled, "Okay."

"The look," she said, motioning to me, "I mean it's awesome but I'm not sure it's you."

"This part is me," I said, shrugging, "I like it."

"Okay," she said, frowning, "What about the suicide attempt?"

I looked around and shifted uncomfortably. I frowned as I looked at the shadows, imagining someone hiding within them.

"Why do you have to do things in the most awkward of places?" I asked, looking around again. Though I didn't see anyone, I wouldn't take the chance.

"No one is here," she said, rolling her eyes.

"Well, I'd like to be more discreet," I whispered, annoyed, "Just…follow me."

I began to walk toward the bleachers but she just stood there. I sighed exasperated, "At least, I'm giving you a choice. You pulled me in here against my will, remember?"

She smiled and nodded her head, "True."

She followed me behind the bleachers and I turned to her, "I have to use my gift. I can't risk speaking in here."

"Does this have to do with Jezebel?" Sarah asked, frowning.

"Yes," I said, looking around, "She's here and I don't want her to know certain things."

She nodded and I placed my hand below my lips, pursing them as I did and blew out the memories. I lowered my hand and waited as the light was inhaled by Sarah. Her eyes widened. I waited as the light faded.

She surprised me by grabbing my wrist, "Jezebel did this?"

I nodded, "And please don't start with the apologies. I get it. You're sorry. If you still feel guilty, help me do what needs to be done."

She nodded and then, grinned, "What do you need me to do?"

"Right now," I said, "Keep everything you have seen to yourself. Tomorrow though, I may need you to help me prove that someone is possessed."

"Do I get to use my gift?" she asked, excited.

"I'll make sure you do," I said, laughing at her enthusiasm.

"Then, I'm in," She said, jumping up and down.

I laughed but inside I slumped over in relief. Everything was coming together. Jezebel's downfall was closer than ever.

****

After school, I found Ky waiting for me by my locker looking sad even though he gave me one of his beautiful half-grins. I frowned as I approached him, sensing the beginning whisper of a warning sounding deep in my soul.

"What's wrong?" I asked, tilting my head to the

side and trying to hide my worry.

"Mom," he whispered, losing his smile, "She's not doing well today."

I swallowed afraid I would tear up and make him worry more, "I'm sorry," I croaked, "I wish there was something I could do."

He shook his head, "Alex, you can't save everyone," he said,shrugging, "I hope you know that," He reached forward and caressed my cheek, "I will be so glad when this Jezebel stuff is over with. It would be nice to kiss my girlfriend and not worry that someone will see."

"It will be nice," I said, giving him a genuine smile.

He looked around and leaned close, "I think I'll sneak a quick one now," he said, pressing his lips to mine quickly.

I took a deep breath as he pulled away wishing the kiss had lasted longer. He caressed my cheek again, "I'm going to drive you home. I will be at the meeting but afterwards…"

"I understand," I said, looking into his beautiful eyes, "Do you want me to come with you?"

"I do," he said, sadly, "But my dad wants just family there for now."

"Okay," I said as we began to walk toward his car.

He opened the door and then, he smiled at me, "Thanks for understanding everything. I don't think I would be able to deal as well if you were mad at me for leaving you alone all the time."

"You're welcome," I said and then, shook my head, "She's your mother but I love her too and she needs her son right now and you need her."

He nodded his head as we got into his car. It was silent as we drove to my house. When we got there my brothers, sister Leighton, Jenna and Sarah were already sitting in the living room.

Jonathon grinned, "So, Sarah knows now?"

"Yep," I said, smiling widely, "And Clyde, Gloria and Drake will know by the end of the day."

"Who does that leave?" Jeremy asked.

"Will, Raina and Daniel," I said, frowning, "Obviously, I'm not telling Daniel because he won't believe me. Then, he'll ruin our plans. If I tell Will too soon, he will tell Daniel and the same thing will happen. So, obviously Raina will know next.

"Do you know who is supposed to defeat Jezebel yet?" Kelly asked, frowning.

"No, I don't," I said with a sigh, "Though I'm sure I'll find out before we face her. My gift has a habit of giving that information right before we fight the demon."

"It does do that, doesn't it?" Jeremy asked, grinning, "I wonder why."

"Me too," I said, rolling my eyes.

The door opened and we all turned to find Drake and Gloria walking into the living room. My heart lurched at the tears running down Gloria's face. She was a beautiful woman with long blonde hair and bright blue eyes that could see into your soul. At least her gift made you feel that way. If she touched you, she would know everything about you. Thankfully, I had learned how to block her gift just like I had Jace's.

Her husband, Drake stood beside her with a look of complete remorse resting in his face. His native american heritage showed in his appearance with his mahogany tinted skin, black hair and brown eyes. For most of my life, he had been possessed by the demon, Asmodis. Thankfully, that possession had ended when we defeated the demon returning him to his life as Gloria's husband, Lynne's father and a member of the Appointed with the gift of super hearing.

I looked at the door expecting to find Clyde but he wasn't there. I frowned at Gloria and she nodded as if she understood who I was looking for, "He's with Lynne and Bastian. They already told him."

"It's a good thing Lynne hasn't been around Daniel," I said, frowning, "Someone needs to remind her what the meaning of secret is before she tells all of ours."

"I know," Gloria said as the door opened.

"Know what?" Lynne asked as she stepped inside holding Bastian's hand.

"The meaning of the word secret," I said with raised brows.

"Don't get your panties in a twist," she said, narrowing her eyes, "Clyde's not mad. His feelings are hurt that you didn't tell him right away."

I sighed, "That's one of the reasons why I wanted to tell him," I said, annoyed.

She shrugged, "You can still explain."

I closed my eyes and shook my head. Finally, the door opened, causing me to open my eyes. Clyde ducked inside. I studied him, warily. Clyde was big...really big. He stood at six feet four inches and his body was covered in rope after rope of muscle. His hair was black and his eyes were almost the same color. Piercings covered his ears. He also had one in his eyebrow, one in his nose and one in his labret. To strangers, he may be terrifying to face but to anyone who knew him, he was a big teddy bear.

"You should have told me," he stated plainly but somehow those words still had the power to make me feel ashamed.

"I was going to," I said and shook my head, "You know how this works. I have to do it when it's time."

"I understand that but it still sucks. Is there anything else you haven't told me?" he asked and I looked at Lynne. She shook her head.

"No," I said, softly, "Other than, don't tell Daniel or Will."

"I know," he said, going to the couch and sitting down, "That would be stupid anyway. Daniel will stop you and Will would help him."

I gave a short laugh, "Exactly."

"Why did you call the meeting, Alex?" Bastian asked, gaining my attention.

"As I told you, I think I might know who Jezebel's host is. I need to know if there is a way to tell if someone is demon possessed?"

Bastian pursed his lips and frowned, "Who do you think it is?"

I shifted uncomfortably, knowing they could think I was jealous but hoping they wouldn't, "Renee."

"Daniel's girlfriend?" Lynne asked, suspiciously.

"It's not because she's his girlfriend," I said, frustrated. I was not jealous and I didn't need them thinking that I was, "It's because of something she said."

"What was it?" Bastian asked as he studied me,

"She said, she likes to see me in pain. It reminded

me of Jezebel. She said I would know every bit of her pain when she gave me these," I said raising my wrist up to show my scars.

Bastian still looked doubtful and I groaned, "Will the test hurt her?" I asked, throwing my hands up.

"Only if she has a demon," Bastian said and smiled finally nodding his head, "If you really think this is a possibility then, I guess it's worth a try. I think we really shouldn't second guess you considering our track record isn't great."

"Thanks," I said, relieved and turned to the others.

"Will everyone be willing to help me do this?" I asked. Slowly, everyone nodded their heads in agreement.

I smiled relieved, "Thank you."

"What's the test?" I asked Bastian.

"You just have to touch her with holy water on your hand," he said, frowning, "I know it sounds simple but if Renee is housing a demon, it'll burn the spot you touched. However, demons can sense holy water if you're really close. You'll have to get close and touch her before she senses it."

I nodded, "Can you find me some holy water?"

"I'll get some tonight," Bastian said, "You'll have your holy water tomorrow morning."

"Then maybe we'll know where Jezebel is by the end of the school day tomorrow," I said, feeling real hope for the first time.

Chapter Fourteen
Standing Together

Catherine met me in the parking lot of the school where the bus dropped us off the next morning. She smiled, sweetly as I walked up to her.

"Lynne called me and told me what's going on today," she said, "I thought you might need my help.

"You thought correctly," I said with a grin, "Did they tell you everything?"

"Did you hear me say it was Lynne that told me?" She asked with a short laugh, "Of course I know everything. I think you should know that Raina now knows everything too. Lynne couldn't hide it from her anymore."

"That was meant to happen," I said, looking into Catherine's eyes, "Where are Lynne and Sarah?"

"They're waiting at the front of the school," Catherine said, scanning the area near the front doors and pointing, "There they are."

Lynne and Sarah were standing beneath a tree that shaded the front entrance of the high school. I waved at them as we walked closer. Lynne grinned and ran to me. She gave me a knowing look before she hugged me, slipping the vial of holy water into my jacket pocket.

"This was left over from Reverend Boothe's stash," she whispered in my ear, "Maybe he'll help us get this done."

I nodded as she pulled away. Slowly, I looked around, finally finding Renee walking with Daniel. I put my hand in my pocket and retrieved the vial, taking it out and pouring it on my hands quickly before dropping it back into my pocket.

I waited until Renee passed and stepped behind her at enough of a distance that she would not be able to sense the holy water. Then, I looked at Sarah and nodded my head as I moved closer.

"I'll be right back," she said with a wide grin as I stepped closer to Renee. I smiled as she walked to the bathroom. A few seconds later, screams erupted. Everyone turned and Lynne purposely knocked me backwards, though to everyone else it looked like an accident. I fell grasping for Renee's bare shoulder and connecting as I used her to steady myself.

I looked up at her as if surprised, watching her eyes cloud in pain. She clasped her hand over her shoulder as her face reddened in anger.

"I'm sorry," I said innocently as she narrowed her eyes.

134.

"You bitch," she said as Daniel looked at each of us confused. Catherine shook her head catching Renee's eyes. Renee's eyes widened so far, they nearly engulfed her face. Still, she stepped toward me but a strange hissing sounded behind me, stopping her. I turned to find a sleek, black snack coiled and ready to strike Renee. Every instinct told me to run even though I knew that the snake was only Sarah. Renee stepped back and turned, running toward the office with Daniel following behind her confused.

Catherine moved closer to me, "Are you okay?"

"Yeah. Did you see her shoulder?" I asked Catherine and Lynne as the snake slithered back to the girl's bathroom amidst screams and panic. They nodded their heads and smiled. A few moments later, Sarah exited the bathroom.

"It's okay," she said loudly to everyone else surrounding us, "I got the snake to go out the window."

I grinned as she joined me, whispering, "You make a good snake."

"I do, don't I?" She asked, proudly and then, looked around searching for Renee, "So what was the verdict?"

"Renee's shoulder was burned," I said, softly, "So, that means Renee is possessed by Jezebel," I raised my brows and smiled, "That means I need for you to tell all of the Appointed except for Daniel to meet me at my house after school and you need to make sure Will is there but don't tell him about the meeting."

"I'll talk to Clyde," Lynne said, grinning, "He'll make sure he's there. He won't know there *is* a meeting until he shows up."

"Excellent," I said and pursed my lips as I saw Renee. Her hand was clasped over her shoulder. Her eyes met mine and I smiled.

She mouthed, "You're dead."

I mouthed back, "No...you are."

****

I sat in Ky's car as he drove me home after school. He glanced at me worried as his mouth set in a grim line. His face reddened as he glanced at me again.

I sighed and closed my eyes, knowing his fear was because of Renee's threat, "Alex, I don't want to leave you by yourself," He said as we pulled into my driveway.

"You need to be with your mom," I said, feeling my heart clench, "I'll be alright. Everyone else will be here. She won't be able to do anything."

"Have you looked at your wrists lately?" He asked, turning to me, "She could hurt you. Alex, she could kill you."

My breath hitched at the fear in his voice, "I'm more careful than I was then," I said, reaching up and caressing his cheek, "I promise. I won't be alone."

"Alex, I can't take the chance," he said, shaking his head, "I-I can't lose you."

"You're not going to lose me," I said and then, smiled, "My brothers and sister aren't going to let anything happen to me. Neither are the rest of the Appointed."

"Your brothers were here the last time," he said, frowning.

"And we didn't know she was going to do that," I said, pursing my lips, "We had no idea she was capable of doing that without a host. Now, we're more careful."

He looked at me doubtful, "Alex, I know you think I'm being over protective but I'm just scared."

"I know," I whispered and then, looked into his eyes, "But there will always be danger. You can't be with me twenty four hours a day. You'll have to trust me to take care of myself and I'll have to trust you to do the same."

He pressed his lips together and nodded, "You're right," he said, looking toward the house, "I'll stay for the meeting and go to my mom afterwards."

I nodded and then, got out of the car as another car pulled up. I raised my eyebrows as a large truck parked behind Ky's car.

"Clyde and Will are here," Ky said as two more cars pulled in the front driveway.

"So are Catherine and Jace," I said, frowning at the other car, "And Lynne and Bastian."

I smiled weakly at Ky and got out of the car to face Will. I knew he would be angry or hurt but I was hoping he would understand why I didn't tell him.

Will got out of the car and walked over to me. From the look on his face, Clyde had told him everything and he was not happy with me. I glanced at Clyde who looked ashamed and then, faced Will again.

"You know I can keep a secret," he said, narrowing his eyes at me, "I haven't told everyone I can stop time and I haven't told them about everyone else's gifts either."

"Daniel is your best friend," I said, raising my eyebrows, "There's a difference between keeping a secret from him and keeping one from everyone else. If you thought he was in danger, you *would* tell him."

"*Is* he in danger?" Will asked, frowning.

"Yes," I whispered, "But only if you tell. I'm doing this the only way he can be saved. If we go any other path he will lose his soul. Jezebel's got her claws into him and he'll do just about anything for her."

"Daniel still loves you too," he said, narrowing his eyes at Ky, "You know that, don't you?"

"Yes," I whispered, "But it *is* over."

He opened his mouth to argue but Lynne came around Bastian's car to stand between us. She looked at us, warily.

"Will, Alex did what was best and we need to start the meeting. The quicker we get this done, the quicker Daniel will be safe," she said, frowning. I nodded as I followed Lynne inside. I looked around realizing everyone was there right before pain slammed through my head. I felt Ky's hand steady me as I screamed out. Slowly, a vision floated in front of my eyes, showing me the one thing I had been waiting to see. I blinked and it faded but as I looked up I understood something I hadn't before. I saw how Jezebel would be defeated....and I knew who would do it.

******

The meeting ended with everyone in attendance knowing what would take place during Jezebel's downfall. Will left with the promise that he wouldn't tell Daniel. However, there was a possibility that he still would. I could only hope Will's sense of loyalty would keep him from betraying the rest of the Appointed's trust.

I watched as everyone else but Raina and Ky followed Will out of the door to go to their homes for the night. Raina talked with my brothers and sister as Ky

138.

pulled me into my room and closed the door. A frown crossed his face.

He caressed my cheek gently as worry clouded his eyes, "Promise me you'll be careful after I leave," he whispered as he leaned down and kissed me. I leaned into him and wrapped my arms around his neck.

"I'll be careful," I whispered against his lips.

He pulled away from me and looked down into my face as if afraid he wouldn't see me again.

"Ky, I promise I'll be careful," I said again forcing a smile, "I'll even call you tonight before I go to bed."

"Okay," he whispered as he looked at the door. When he looked back at me he seemed torn, "Call me if anything…bad happens."

"Okay," I said, nodding, "I will."

He grinned and pulled me to him once more, kissing me deeply. He pulled away, leaving me alone once again as he left to go back to his mother. A few minutes later Raina came into my room. She stood in the center of the room staring at me. Finally, she rolled her eyes.

"I can't say I love the look," she said and then, shrugged, "But you are still you…right?"

I smiled, "Of course. Just because I dress differently doesn't mean I'm not in here. I'm still basically the same."

She nodded before shifting nervously, "It must have hurt to have us all ignoring you…but in my defense I didn't know what to say. I was always afraid I'd send you over the edge again."

"Don't worry," I said, giving a short laugh, "I had therapy."

She laughed with me, "I see your ability to spew sarcasm hasn't changed."

"Nothing else has changed but my clothes…and my boyfriend," I said, shrugging.

"You mean…You're single, right?" She asked, frowning. She narrowed her eyes at me and then, grinned, "You're seeing Ky, aren't you?"

I winced, wondering if there was a way to lie to her but when I looked at her I saw there wasn't, "Please don't tell anyone yet," I pleaded, "I don't want drama to take our attention away from Jezebel and I don't want her to hurt him. Look what she's doing to Daniel."

Raina smiled, "I won't tell anyone," she said and gave me a sweet, reassuring smile, "He seems to be good for you."

"He is," I whispered, relieved that she saw that.

"That's all I want is for you to be happy," she said and tilted her head. She seemed to be considering something and then, nodded her head as she made a decision, "So, since we're swapping secrets, I thought I'd tell you, I'm dating your brother."

My eyes widened, "Which one?"

"Jonathon's a little too young, don't you think?" She asked, laughing, "Jeremy….I'm dating Jeremy."

"Why didn't you tell me?" I asked, frowning. It seemed strange to keep their relationship a secret.

"We didn't know how you or anyone else would take it," she said with a shrug.

"Well, I think it's cool," I said and laughed, "My brother couldn't end up with a better person."

"I'm glad you're happy about it," she said and shifted uncomfortably as she changed the subject, "I heard what happened with your dad."

I nodded and bit my lip, "It was a surprise," I said and frowned, "It makes me wonder if his drug problem is my fault since it's his guilt over me having the gift that causes him to drink and do drugs."

Raina pursed her lips and shook her head, "Everyone's problems are their own fault. He lets it get to him. You embrace your gift. It may cause you problems but you do what's right."

I nodded, "Yeah, I guess," I said and then, gave a short laugh, "But I feel bad."

"You always feel bad," she said, shaking her head, "You're just sensitive that way."

"I guess I am," I said, laughing, "Would it surprise you to find out I felt sorry for Jezebel when I read about her relationship with Asmodis?"

"It doesn't surprise me, but as your friend, I have to advise you to let that go," she said, smiling, "Don't let your feelings about her past keep you from doing what needs to be done."

"I won't," I said, shaking my head, "I can't. Otherwise Daniel will lose his soul and she will eventually kill me after killing every single one of you."

She frowned at me, "That would be a disaster."

"Worse than a disaster," I said, frowning, "It would be the end of the world."

Chapter Fifteen
Good-byes

I was laying in my bed, listening to my radio when my cell phone began to ring. I frowned as I looked toward the clock finding that it was eight o'clock at night. I pursed my lips as I picked up my phone. I looked at the caller I.D. and smiled. It was Ky. He had called me thirty minutes earlier than usual. I pushed the button and answered the phone. Instantly, my smile died as Ky's sobs came to me from the other end of the line. My heart froze in my chest as I inhaled, sharply.

"Ky, what's wrong?" I asked, alarmed but a part of me already knew the answer to that question.

"It's mom," he whispered, "She stopped breathing. They were able to get her to breathe again but they don't think she's going to make it through the night. Alex, please get here. I don't think I can do this by myself."

142.

My eyes teared up as I swallowed over the lump in my throat. I took a deep breath, pushing the soul crushing grief away.

"I'll be there," I said, getting out of bed and seeing Kelly look at me with a question in her eyes, "I'll make sure the others know too."

"Hurry," he whispered, "Please."

"I will," I said going to my closet and pulling out my clothes, "I will be there as soon as I can."

He sobbed again and then, the phone went dead. I looked toward Kelly who was sitting on her bed. A tear escaped my eye.

"What is it?" Kelly asked, alarmed.

I pressed my lips together, not wanting to speak the words but knowing I would have to. Finally, I forced my lips apart, "Micah, is in the hospital," I said, feeling the tears make hot trails down my cheeks, "The doctors don't think she'll make it through the night."

Kelly swallowed hard as tears instantly streamed down her face, "I'm going."

A new worry pierced my heart as I took in my sister's heart-broken appearance, "This isn't your fault," I said, warily, "Your gift wouldn't allow you to save her because it's her time."

"I understand that," she said, blinking another tear from her eye, "But it sucks. I just wish I could do something. It makes me angry that I can't."

"It's okay to feel angry. That's normal," I said, frowning. She gave me a sad smile and nodded. I forced a smile back, "Get dressed. I'm going to get Jeremy and Jonathon and I'm going to tell mom."

"Okay," she whispered as I left the room.

Ten minutes later, we were piled into Jeremy's car. My mother followed us in hers. I made the calls to every one of the Appointed as Jeremy drove to the hospital.

Micah's husband, Culver met us at the entrance of the hospital. As I looked at him, I realized he had gifted his son with most of his looks. He was tall, broad-shouldered with black hair and indigo eyes. Tears fell down his cheeks freely but he managed to smile at us as we walked up to him.

"Alex," he said in a voice so sad it hurt my chest to hear it, "I'm so glad you've come. Ky needs you now."

"I've called everyone else," I said and looked behind me, "My brothers and sister are with me. So, is my mom."

He nodded and motioned toward the door. He stopped at the front desk and talked to the nurse allowing her to permit the others to a waiting room outside of Micah's room.

"I'm going to tell Ky you're here," he whispered and I nodded my head as he entered Micah's room.

Almost immediately Ky emerged from the room, looking pale and panicked. Automatically, he engulfed me in a hug, surprising my family with it's intensity. Slowly, he lifted his head from my shoulder and looked toward my mother and Kelly.

"She wants to see you," he said as a tear fell down his cheek. He looked at me, "She'll see us last."

I nodded, swallowing over the knot in my throat. I held Ky's hand silently as we stood outside Micah's room waiting for my mother and Kelly to exit. Slowly, the rest of the Appointed arrived. Finally, my mother and Kelly emerged from the room with tears running freely down their faces.

I watched as each of the others arrived. They filed in and then, out of the room where Micah lay dying. Her husband and Aubrey went in before Ky and myself. I trembled with dread as my time to see Micah for what I knew would be the final time would come. Finally, they emerged. Culver was holding Aubrey close to him as he looked toward us and nodded.

Slowly, we walked toward the room. I trembled not knowing what to say or do. I had never said good-bye to someone who was dying.

When we entered the room, I found Micah lying quietly on the bed. Her breathing came weak and shallow.

"Alex," she breathed with a smile on her pale lips.

"Micah," I said going to her and grabbing her hand. The words caught in my throat and I had to take a couple of deep breaths.

"It's okay," she said, motioning to the chair, "Don't be sad. I'll be with Reverend Boothe and his beautiful wife soon and I'll be with my dad and mom."

"But we'll miss you," I said, crying fully now, "Every single day, we'll miss you."

"But you don't need to," she said with a soft smile, "I'll be with you always."

I nodded but could feel a presence behind me. I turned to find Semerias. My mouth opened in shock.

"What are you doing here?" I asked and Ky frowned as he looked behind me.

"I'm here to make her journey easier," he said, raising his chin.

I looked at Ky, "An angel…Semerias is here," I

said, feeling my heart-break, "He's here to…help her."

"I see him," Micah said with wide eyes.

"Call her family in one last time," Semerias said, softly.

I nodded and went to the door as Micah's chest rose and fell in quick succession. I called everyone in.

Semerias looked around the room, "She has been blessed with so much love," he said, smiling, "That is a beautiful legacy."

I nodded unable to answer him with my mother, Culver and Aubrey in the room. I walked back to the bed to stand beside Micah as she looked at each of us. Her breaths were sporadic.

"Thank…you…for….loving…me," she whispered, "Don't…cry for…me. I'll be…safe…and I'll make…sure…you are. I…love…you…all…so…much."

"We love you too," her daughter cried.

"I know," she said and then, smiled toward Semerias, "This…is not…good-bye. I'll be….there waiting for you."

Then, her eyes closed and the line on the heart monitor went flat. A sob broke from her daughter's throat.

"Momma!" She screamed, "Please, please come back! Please!"

Her father took her in his arms as Ky sank beside his mother on the other side of Micah's bed and sobbed. Slowly, I knelt beside him and took him in my arms. He laid his head on my chest and sobbed. I looked up at Semerias and saw Micah standing beside him looking like she had when she was healthy. She smiled.

"Take care of him," she said, reaching forward and

touching him with one ghostly hand.

I nodded as I hugged Ky closer to me. I closed my eyes knowing that I didn't even have to make the promise because I loved him. I truly loved hm.

****

I sat in the waiting room with Lynne as I watched Ky and his father speak to the doctor. My heart lurched as I saw how broken Ky was over his mother's death. I had stayed after everyone but family had left. Even my mother and siblings were gone. Still, I didn't understand what I could do for Ky. My presence didn't seem to be enough.

"Alex," Lynne whispered. I pulled my gaze from Ky and looked at Lynne.

She seemed to be fighting to find words. Finally, she closed her eyes and inhaled before looking at me again, "You and Ky aren't just friends, are you?"

I looked back at him, knowing that I couldn't lie about our relationship to his family. Slowly, I shook my head and then, met her eyes, "No, we're not just friends," I whispered, "We just didn't want anyone to know until after we defeated Jezebel."

"Why?" She asked, frowning as she studied my face.

"A few reasons," I said, and bit my lip nervously, "The first and most important reason is I'm worried Jezebel will come after him. She wants to hurt me and she's already come after Daniel. If she finds out how much I love Ky, she'll go after him."

"Love?" she asked raising her brows, surprised.

"Yes, I love him," I whispered, "I know it sounds weird. Everyone is used to me being with Daniel and I will always love him but I'm in love with Ky."

"I don't think it sounds weird," she said, looking toward him, "He is good for you and you're good for him and my cousin needs that. Even though we are used to seeing you with Daniel…we can get used to seeing you with Ky."

I leaned over and hugged her relieved, "I love you so much, Lynne."

She gave a short laugh, "Of course you do. What's not to love?"

She pulled back and smiled sadly, "You did tell Micah that you were with him?"

"Of course," I said as I looked toward the room where her body laid. The flat line on the heart monitor was finally silent, "I didn't want her to pass without knowing."

"That makes me happy," she said, giving a short laugh, "At least she knew Ky wouldn't be alone."

I smiled but looked back into her eyes, "I am asking that you still keep our relationship a secret to keep him safe and also, I don't want anything to take away the focus on Jezebel. Though you accept our relationship the others may not." I said, softly and looked toward Ky again.

She nodded, "You're talking about Daniel?"

"I am," I said and rolled my eyes, "He's voiced how much he doesn't approve."

She scoffed, "He really doesn't have a right to tell you who you can or can not date," she said and then, rolled her eyes, "But I do see your point. I will keep your relationship a secret until Jezebel is sent back to hell."

"As soon as that happens, you can tell everyone," I

148.

said, smiling, "I'm actually looking forward to that secret being exposed."

"Well, you know I don't mind telling everyone," she said, grinning, "I'll be dying to tell them by that time."

"I know you will," I said, laughing.

She frowned and tilted her head, "So, the childhood romance is over and your starting something new…"

"Yes on both counts. The truth is I'll always care about Daniel," I said, "And I'll always love him in some way but he made his choice and it wasn't me. Now, I'm making my choice to be with someone else too…someone who was there for me when no one else was and even better, someone who loves me back as much as I love him."

Lynne nodded her head and hugged me again, "You deserve that," she whispered, "Be happy…and make him happy too. Just remember to make time with your best friend."

"I will," I said as she released me and stood. She gave me a smile and I looked toward Ky. He turned to me and I felt the sudden shift of change in my life and all I could see in my future was him.

Chapter Sixteen
Ashes to Ashes

I stood in front of a hole dug into the ground in an open field. Stone markers were placed every few feet. The sky overhead, was dark grey though it did not rain. A part of me wondered if Micah was telling the angels not to cry…that she was happy. It would be like her.

The preacher's sermon fell upon my ears with the normal details of her life. Then, it was her family's turn to speak. Her husband stepped forward wearing a dark blue suit and yellow and blue pinstriped tie.

He looked at each of his children before he spoke. Tears rested in his indigo eyes. I stood beside Ky, holding his hand in comfort as his father spoke of the woman who had loved him more than her own life.

His voice was tear roughened as he spoke, "My wife loved everyone. She talked about everyone here with so much love and so much worry…and care. She prayed for each of you every night. To our children, she was the best mother. I have no idea how we will do without her," he said, beginning to sob, "But we will go on because that's what she would want us to do…go on and thrive. She'd want us to be happy," he looked toward the coffin placed over the hole it would soon fill, "I love you, my beautiful angel…always."

I swallowed over the lump in my throat as Ky released my hand. I wished I could stand beside him as he spoke. I wish I could give him comfort in my presence as he took his father's place at the head of the casket. His eyes found the coffin and coughed over what I was sure was tears and looked at me as he spoke.

"My mother taught me strength. She told me to always do what I thought was right…even if it wasn't the popular idea. She taught me to be protective of those I love and she taught me how to laugh. I know mom watches over me. I know she still loves me and she loves every one of you too," he said, as tears fell down his cheeks, "And even though I understand she's irreplaceable, I hope I can carry on her legacy in a way that would make her proud. I hope you will help me do that."

His sobs broke from him as he stepped from the head of the casket and touched the wooden top, "I love you, mom," he whispered and came to stand next to me with his head bowed. Slowly, I reached forward and grabbed his hand. He gripped it tightly in his as if afraid to let go.

Aubrey was the next to speak. I gave her a smile in encouragement as she stood shaking in front of everyone. Her sweet, innocent voice rose only slightly as she began, "Mom was beautiful," She said, softly, "Even while she was on this earth, she was an angel. She was my best friend and loved me even when I felt no one did. I still have everyone else but the love my mother gave me was different. I will always miss her and I will always love her. Always."

She stepped down and touched the casket, "I love you, Momma."

Drake stepped forward, caressing the casket of his beloved sister and blew it a kiss. He looked at us with tears, falling down his face as he spoke, "Micah was a kind and beautiful woman but she was also a teacher. One of the things she taught me was that people take the past for granted but it is very important. It teaches us not to make the same mistakes over and over," he said as tears fell down his cheeks, "Now, the past is where she will always live. That is where we loved her best and we hugged her and kissed her and made wonderful memories. It's what I will always hold in my heart. I love you, Micah."

The preacher took his place at the head of the casket again. As the prayer began I could hear Renee who was standing beside Daniel beginning to complain, "Can we go now?" She whispered a little too loud.

I opened my eyes and narrowed them at her, trying to remind myself that she was possessed. Still, she continued and I began to become upset with Daniel for bringing her. As soon as the preacher said amen, Daniel and Renee were walking toward his car. I shook my head as Lynne came to stand next to me and Ky.

"I wish I could send her back to hell right now,"

Lynne said, frowning, "Especially since she was disrespectful at my aunt's funeral."

"She's a demon, Lynne," I said, frowning, "You didn't really expect her to be respectful of one of the Appointed, did you?"

"No, but I did expect for Daniel to leave her at home," She said, shaking her head, "I told him only the Appointed and family."

"Like he'll listen right now," I said, shaking my head, "You know that's not going to happen. My god, Lynne. He told her all of our secrets."

"Yes, he did," She said, through gritted teeth. Her eyes narrowed dangerously, "So, when are we supposed to defeat the little witch?"

"Well, that's where I feel disrespectful. I'm pretty sure Micah would understand though," I said, frowning. I winced as I spoke the next words, "We need to have a meeting today. Can you get everyone but Daniel to my house?"

"If it means she will be gone, then yes," Lynne said, watching as Daniel started his car and drove away.

"Then, it will happen tonight," I said, softly.

"Good," she said, frowning when I took out my cellphone.

"Who are you calling?" She asked, confused.

"I'm calling my dad," I said, dialing the number, "I'm giving him a choice to do what's right. I'm telling him what is going to happen and he can show up and help us or not."

She nodded as I dialed the last digit of his phone number, "Then, I'll leave you to it."

I nodded as my father answered the phone,

"Daddy," I said into the phone, "I think it's time for you to decide what to do…."

****

Everyone arrived at my house soon after leaving the cemetery. My mother still had to go to work and had only returned home to change. I had decided to allow Ky to drive me back to my house, arriving a few minutes after my brothers and sister. The others followed us in.

Ky sat next to me quietly on my couch, holding my hand in his. I had decided that I didn't care if anyone saw me holding his hand because Jezebel's defeat was so close that it wouldn't matter and more importantly, he needed me right now. Tears still fell down his face as everyone waited for my mother to leave. I watched him feeling helpless yet again. What could I do to comfort him?

My mother left after giving more tear-filled condolences to Ky. Everyone sighed in relief as they heard her car start and pull out of the driveway.

Sarah turned to me, "Please tell me, this is going down tonight," She said, angrily, "Because I don't think I can keep from turning into a tiger so that I can rip Renee limb from limb."

"Please don't do that. It's definately happening tonight," I assured her, nodding my head, "But it has to be exact and to make sure that happens, I have to show you all again to make sure you know what your supposed to do."

Everyone but Ky groaned. He looked at me confused, "I have to use my gift," I explained.

"Does it hurt?" He asked, looking around at everyone.

154.

"No," Jonathon said, "But it does feel strange."

"Okay," he said, warily, "If this will help, do it."

I nodded and put all of my visions about how to defeat Jezebel into my mind. I put my hand in front of me and blew out. The whole room filled with light so bright that I had to close my eyes against its intensity. Slowly, the glow pulsed and faded.

"Does everyone think they can do what needs to be done?" I asked, a few minutes later.

"Yes," they said in unison.

"Then, all we can do is wait," I said with a shrug, "Does anyone want a soda?"

Everyone raised their hands. I sighed as I turned and walked toward the kitchen with Ky behind me. He was oddly quiet. Slowly, I turned to face him.

"Are you going to be okay with this?" I asked, frowning, "We just buried your mom."

"My worries have nothing to do with my mom," he said, stepping closer to me.

"So, what are you worried about?" I asked, searching his face.

He frowned as he looked into my eyes, "When Daniel goes back to being Daniel, I'm worried you won't want me anymore. You'll want to be with him."

My mouth opened in shock, "Ky, I promise you that won't happen," I said as I caressed his cheek, "I'm not going to leave you."

"How do you know that?" He asked as another tear fell from his eye.

"Because I know how I feel," I said as my heart broke.

"I hope you're right," he said as a sob broke from

his throat, "Because I can't deal with this alone. I can't be…without you."

"You won't have to be alone. I'll be right there," I said as I hugged him close. I closed my eyes as he held on to me for what seemed to be hours…afraid to let go….afraid he would lose me.

Chapter Seventeen
Past and Present

The park had always been surprisingly big for such a small town. For the most part it held good memories. I had played there with every member of the Appointed. I had been a child then and though I was nearly grown and our mission had brought us there for battle, it somehow felt right to wage our war there. It felt like a passage way to growing up.

We walked through the thick foliage that surrounded the play area and came to a dirt road. Quietly, we walked down the wide dirt road until we found Daniel's car.

I had known how I would find Daniel when the time came to cast the demon away since the day Micah and Ky had come to visit me at Running River though I did not know we would be casting the demon out of the one he was with. Still, I could feel the pang in my heart as I saw his naked body thrusting against hers. I shifted, uncomfortable and looked away.

Ky leaned close to me with worry and concern written clearly on his face, "Are you okay?"

"Yes," I said in disgust, "I just didn't want to see that."

"None of us did," Lynne grumbled, looking anywhere but at the car.

I looked at Clyde, "You know what to do," I said, motioning to the car.

Clyde nodded . He walked to the back of the car and leaned down, grabbing the bumper with one hand. He lifted the back-end of the car as easily as if he were picking up a leaf. I watched in awe as he moved the car up and down and left to right before he dropped it unceremoniously to the ground. A few seconds later, I heard Daniel cursing.

I heard rustling and a couple of curse words before the car door opened. Daniel exited wearing only his jeans. Renee was behind him, straightening her dress. When she saw me, she grinned.

"Did you put him up to this?" Daniel asked taking two menacing steps before seeing Ky step beside me protectively.

"Yes, I did," I said, raising my chin.

"Why?" He asked, narrowing his eyes, "Is it because you're jealous, Alex? You are crazy. Maybe you should have stayed a bit longer in the hospital."

I curled my hands into fists wanting to hit him. Instead, my face reddened, "You're so conceited," I said, angrily, "Have you ever thought this has something to do with the Appointed."

He frowned as he looked around finally noticing the rest of the Appointed surrounding his car. He looked back at me, confused.

"What are you talking about, Alex?" He asked as his eyes shifted to each of the Appointed.

"You're girlfriend is possessed by Jezebel," I said, frowning as Renee rolled her eyes, "She only chose to be with you to hurt me."

He grinned, "No, you're lying," he said, shaking his head in denial. He lost his grin as he looked into my face. He turned to Renee, "Tell them you're not Jezebel."

She gave him a half grin and cocked a brow, "But if I told them that, it would be a lie and I'm not that type of demon."

His eyes widened as he backed away from her, "No," he said, shaking his head, "Your joking…This is a joke, right?"

"No one is joking. She's Jezebel, Daniel," Lynne said, "If you need proof, look at her shoulder. It's burned where we touched her with holy water."

Daniel's eyes widened as he faced Renee again, "I thought you said, that was a chemical burn from hair dye," he said, breathing fast.

"Okay," she grinned, "So, I do lie….a lot. Like when I said I noticed your eyes first. That was a lie. I noticed you were hers," she said pointing at me, "You have always been my favorite tool of revenge against her."

Daniel looked at me pained, "Tell me this isn't

true, Alex."

"I can't," I whispered as my chest tightened at the pain in his eyes.

"How long have you known?" He asked stepping closer to me. I shifted. Even after everything he had done to me, I didn't want to hurt him. Still, he wanted the truth.

"I suspected that Renee was possessed since the day you told her all of the Appointed's secrets," I said, raising my chin, "I've known for sure since I touched her with the holy water."

"And you didn't tell me?" He asked, stepping even closer to me.

"You wouldn't have believed me," I said, shaking my head, "You would have thought I was lying or jealous. You thought that just a few seconds ago."

"But you weren't around when I met her," he said, shaking his head, "You were in the hospital because you tried to commit suicide."

"I didn't try to commit suicide either," I said, tilting my chin toward Renee, "Jezebel slit my wrists."

His mouth dropped open but I turned back to Renee, "I was punished for something I didn't even do."

"What are you talking about?" Renee asked, snarling.

"I didn't send Asmodis back to hell," I said, smiling sweetly, "I was dead at the time."

"No," she said, shaking her head, "You're lying."

"I'm not," I said, raising my brow, "Though I did see his death and tell the others how it was supposed to happen."

"That's enough then," She said angrily.

160.

Before I could move she was charging toward me. A second before she reached me a strong wind hit her, pushing her backwards and into a tree so hard it knocked down several branches. My heart skipped a beat.

I stared at Renee in shock as the wind died down. This had been one part of the plan I was never sure about. I had thought it was impossible.

Slowly, I turned to face a man I had once put on a pedestal.

"Hello, Daddy," I whispered, "Thank you for saving me."

My father smiled for the first time in years and it reached his eyes which were clear of drugs and alcohol. He stepped beside me and whispered, "Any time, Baby Girl."

****

Renee straightened as I turned back to her. Her eyes glowed showing the demon which lived within her. She took a determined step toward me but Kelly blocked her path. She frowned as she looked at my little sister obviously trying to remember which power Daniel had told her she possessed.

Kelly stretched her hand toward Renee and met her eyes just as she took a step backward but it was too late, "Renee, you are healed from the disease of possession," she said in a strong voice, "Jezebel you are ordered out of her body!"

A scream tore from deep in Renee's chest as Jezebel poured from her mouth in a large cloud of red smoke. Daniel's eyes widened as the smoke took the form of Jezebel as I had seen her the very first night in the dream. His mouth dropped open in shock as he stepped back and sank to the ground.

Jezebel turned and looked toward my father and raised her brow, "I remember you now," she said with a grin, "I've helped you get into so much trouble. As a matter of fact, she wouldn't have her gift if I hadn't made you lust for a better life."

I narrowed my eyes as anger raced through my veins hot as lava and just as deadly. She was the reason for my father's guilt...not me. My father grabbed my arm and pulled me behind him.

He raised his chin and faced Jezebel, "Well, think of this as payback for all that trouble."

She laughed, "I'm sorry, Ryan but you'll have to take turns like a good little boy," she purred, "I'm here to play with your daughter."

Then, she rushed toward me but Catherine stepped in front of me, "You feel a deep twisting pain in your stomach," she said, narrowing her eyes and Jezebel bent over groaning in pain but her determination pushed her to move forward.

"You're gift won't save her this time," Jezebel said, gasping as she forced herself to take a step, "This is between me and Alex. She has to pay for killing Asmodis."

I shook my head and then, met her eyes, "I told you, I didn't kill him," I said, raising my brows, "And I won't kill you."

At that moment, she lunged toward me again and my father blew her back once again. Raina stepped forward and Jezebel's eyes widened.

"Meet your killer," I said, as Raina picked up a large sharp stick with her mind and slammed it straight into Jezebel's heart. Jezebel looked at her shocked as she fell to the ground. Jeremy stepped beside her and stretched his hand forward incinerating her into ashes.

I raised my face to the heavens and shouted as loud as I could, "Semerias, close Jezebel's gate."

The earth began to shake in response. I looked around back at where Jezebel had stood. Nothing gave evidence that she had ever even existed. Jezebel was gone.

Chapter Eighteen
Decisions

I rode home with my brothers and sister after Jezebel's defeat instead of riding with Ky. I knew that action worried him but I had to face one more obstacle before my life could begin to be normal again.

As soon as I exited the car I walked up the steps to the deck. My brothers and sister seemed to realize I needed the time alone so they walked to the front door.

I took a deep breath as I looked out over the backyard. It was strange to know I could be there with no danger of Jezebel attacking me. She was truly gone. Slowly, I smiled. I was free…at least for a little while.

I don't know how long I stood there in complete peace with my life before I sensed I was not alone. I didn't turn to face the person who had come to me. Instead, I gave one last longing look at the backyard.

164.

"Alex," I heard Daniel say after a few moments. Slowly, I turned completely breaking the peace that I had experienced.

When I faced him, I found him standing outside the door. His face was so pained that my heart ached. I pressed my lips together as he walked closer to me.

"I'm guessing you don't want me here but I wanted to apologize," he said, as he studied my face. Slowly, he released a shuttering breath, "I've made a mess of everything."

"Yes, you did," I said, not bothering to deny it. I looked behind him, "Where's Renee?"

He lowered his head, ashamed and shrugged before facing me again. He forced his spine straighter.

"She's home. She remembers that we've dated but she doesn't remember anything about Jezebel or the Appointed," he said, shifting uneasily, "And she broke up with me."

"I'm sorry," I whispered, sadly, "I really am."

"Don't be," he said, shrugging, "I would have broken up with her if she hadn't done it first. I really didn't know what was real in our relationship."

"Oh," I said too uncomfortable to say anything else.

The silence stretched as I shifted. Honestly, I wished he would leave but I knew he wasn't done with the conversation.

"Alex, I really have no right to want anything from you," he said and I winced because I knew what was next, "But I...I want you back."

I met his eyes, wishing he hadn't spoken those words. My chin raised as I took a deep breath.

"I'm sorry," I said, shaking my head, "You can't have me back."

He blinked surprised. He had truly expected for me to forgive him for everything and be with him again.

"Why not?" He asked, frowning and then, his eyes widened, "Alex, you can't blame what happened on me. I was under a spell."

"No, you weren't," I said as my heart squeezed, "You chose to be with Renee. Jezebel didn't make you. You didn't want to wait for me. You turned your back on me because you wanted to."

"Then, I made a mistake," he said, pleading now, "And I'm sorry."

"It's still too late," I said as the lump in my throat grew larger, "I've went on with my life. I'm in love with someone else now."

"Ky?" He asked with hurt clear on his face, "He's not good for you."

"Yes," I whispered, "He is. He's been better for me than you have ever been."

"So you choose Ky over me?" He asked stepping forward. His breath shuttered as tears filled his eyes.

"I do," I said, tearing up over the hurt on his face, "I will always choose him."

He nodded once releasing one of the tears to fall down his cheek as he sighed.

"I'm not angry at you," he said with a short laugh, "I can't be when this is my fault but...I can't be here right now. It hurts too much."

"I understand," I whispered and then, he was gone.

I took a deep breath as I cried the tears for him that I had been holding in since returning home. When the tears ran out, I raised my head and took what felt like the first breath I had taken in a long time.

****

I called Ky shortly after my tears ran out. He immediately answered the phone. I took a deep, calming breath as soon as I heard his voice.

"I need for you to come to my house," I whispered, "Will you come?"

"Alex, I'm at your door now," he said, warily, "I've been here for a little while trying to decide what to do."

"Come to the deck," I said, relieved, "I'm there."

"I'm on my way," he said, softly.

A few minutes later, I could hear his heavy footfalls on the deck steps as he climbed to the top. Finally, I saw him.

He looked at me with fear and worry mingling in his eyes. His black hair was sticking up as if he had ran his hands through it repeatedly.

"What happened?" He asked, taking a step toward me and stopping.

"Daniel came to visit me," I said as I watched his face darken. I bit my bottom lip and continued, "Renee broke up with him."

"I expected that," he said, frowning. He tilted his head and swallowed visibly before continuing, "But that's not all is it?"

"No," I said, watching him carefully, "He asked me to come back to him."

Silence stretched for a few moments. He closed his eyes and took a breath before opening them to look at me, "And what did you say?"

I smiled as I stepped close to him, "Well, I told him that I choose you."

He took a deep, relieved breath as he grinned, "You did?"

I gave a short laugh, "Of course I did," I said, caressing his cheek, "Why would you think I wouldn't?"

"Because you were in love with him," he said as his face darkened again.

"I was…but I'm not anymore," I said with a raised brow.

"You're not?" He asked, looking for the truth in my face.

"No because….well, you see I kind of….might….definitely be in love with you," I said, laughing as he leaned closer to me.

He smiled the crooked smile I loved so well and pulled me against him.

"Well, it's a good thing," he said, leaning in toward my ear as he whispered, "Because I kind of…might…definitely be in love with you too."

I smiled at him before I kissed him more passionately than I had ever kissed him before. He kissed me back, making me truly happy once again.

Epilogue

In Hell

Lucifer felt every part of his world shake as Semerias entered Hell. Fear and hate resonated deep within Lucifer as he stared at the angel. White wings spread behind his back giving a beautiful contrast to the flames surrounding him. His eyes burned with complete loathing as he looked upon the angel who had once been like a brother.

Slowly, Semerias folded his wings but that did not take the fact away that he was not someone who should be pushed. Still, Lucifer showed no fear as he faced him.

"What are you doing here?" He asked seeming unphased though the fear was pulsing within him as sure as a heart beat, "Did you decide to join us, Semerias?"

Semerias narrowed his eyes. He had chosen to stay in the heavens when Lucifer had fallen, "I would never join you."

Lucifer narrowed his eyes, "Well, if that's not the reason, why are you here?" He asked, pursing his lips,

"You have to be here for a reason. Otherwise, you wouldn't be allowed."

"I thought you would want this," Semerias said, pushing something which resembled a jewelry box toward him. He studied it, confused.

"What is it?" he asked, frowning.

"What's left of Jezebel," Semerias said with a crooked grin, "This time the Appointed didn't just send her back to you...they killed her. That's never happened before."

Lucifer frowned down at the box, "You interfered," he whispered, "They wouldn't have known how to defeat her unless you told them."

"I didn't interfere," Semerias answered with a smile, "The appointed are well equipped to defeat anything or anyone you send."

Lucifer pursed his lips but Semerias was already leaving, "I just thought you'd like her back home where she belongs."

Then, Semerias was gone. Lucifer picked up the box and opened it releasing the ashes into the air. He slammed his fist into the wall of his lair as a roar burst from his lips.

He looked above him, "I will defeat them all," he said, loudly, "You will not win in this. All of the Appointed will die. I declare war on them...I declare war on all of them!"

With those words the demon hoardes rose, ready to do Lucifer's bidding.

Characters

The Appointed

1.) Alexandra Denton- She has the ability to see the future. She is the sister of Jeremy, Jonathon and Kelly. She is the girlfriend of Daniel.

2.) Catherine Rollins- She has the ability to control others senses. She is the girlfriend of Jace.

3.) Clyde Ramirez- He has the ability to derive super strength from the energy of the earth.

4.) Daniel Wallace- He has the ability to transport from one place to the other with the power of his mind. He is the boyfriend of Alexandra.

5.) Gloria Taylor- She has the ability to know everything about a person or object by touch. She is the wife of Drake. She is the mother of Lynne and the sister-in-law of Micah.

6.) Jace Fairveiw- He has the ability to communicate with only the mind. He is the boyfriend of Catherine.

7.) Jenna Warren- She has the ability to hear extremely long distances.

8.) Jeremy Matten- He has the ability to control fire. He is the brother of Alexandra, Jonathon and Kelly.

9.) Jonathon Matten- He has the ability to control water. He is the brother of Alexandra, Jeremy and Kelly.

10.) Kelly Matten- She has the ability to heal a person as long as the heart is still beating.

11.) Ky Andrews- He is the son of Micah. He is the nephew of Drake and Gloria and cousin to Lynne.

12.) Leighton West- He has the ability to enter another person's dreams or pull them into his.

13.) Lynne Taylor- She has the ability to fly or levitate. She is the daughter of Gloria and Drake. She is the niece of Micah.

14.) Micah Anderson- She has the ability to touch a person and know their pasts. She is the sister of Drake. She is the sister in law of Gloria and aunt of Lynne.

15.)   Raina Simon- She has the ability to move objects with her mind.
16.) Sarah Niles- She has the ability to speak to animals and shape shift.
17.) Will Henson- He has the ability to control time.

The Protectors

1.) Reverend Asa Boothe- He is the elder protector. He is the uncle to Bastian.
2.) Bastian Boothe- He is the younger protector. He is the nephew of Asa.

The Demon and Possessed

1.) Asmodis- He is a high-lord demon of violence.
2.) Drake Taylor- He was originally a member of the appointed but became possessed. He is the husband of Gloria. He is the father of Lynne and the brother of Micah.

Coming to Kindle in October of 2013!

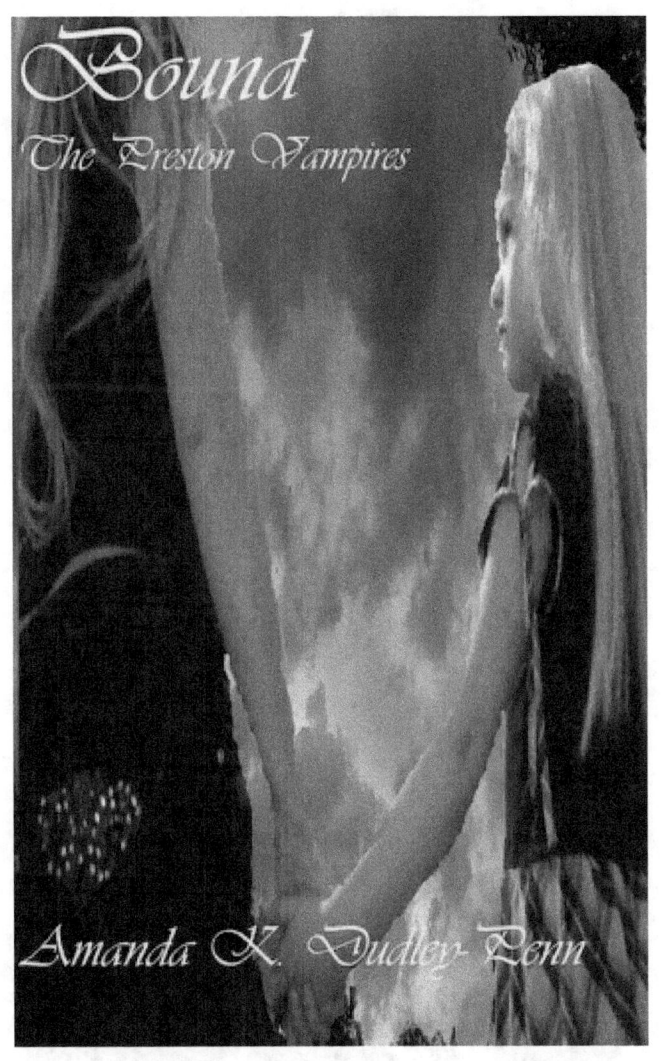

Available on Kindle and Nook!

Available on Kindle and Nook!
The Hidden (Book 1) The Alexandra Denton Chronicles
is also available in paperback!

Now available on Kindle and Nook!
Beckoned (Book 1) The Brazil Werewolf Series is also
available in paperback!!

Amanda K. Dudley-Penn was born in June of 1977 in Tullahoma,
Tennessee. She has loved writing from a very young age and spent her time writing stories and poetry for those close to her. It quickly became her dream to become a published writer. With the support of her three children and husband, she began writing her first novel, The Hidden in 2008 and finished it
in June of 2012. She is currently the author of three series, The Alexandra Denton Chronicles, The Brazil Werewolf Series and The Preston Vampire Series. She currently lives in Grand Prairie, Texas with her husband, David and her children, Constance,

Isabella and Joshua.

www.ingramcontent.com/pod-product-compliance
Lightning Source LLC
Chambersburg PA
CBHW060817120626
46557CB00001B/253